A RISQUÉ ENGAGEMENT

In The Heart of a Valentine Book Two

STEPHANIE NICOLE NORRIS

D1520967

Acknowledgments

Wow, it's been a been a journey writing these stories from my heart, and I want to take a moment to acknowledge a few of you who have been instrumental with helping me through this process.

Special thanks first and foremost to my readers. You guys are amazing, and I love each and every one of you. To my illustrator Amy Q. To be able to take my vision and bring it to my cover is amazing, and I am in awe of you! To my editor Shonell Bacon, your critique is so influential and priceless to me! Thank you for having my back and being a part of my team!

To my literary partner in crime Deidra D. S. Green, you have so many roles I can't name them all. LOL. Thank you for having my back and being my sounding board when I'm crazy and trying to write 50-thousand books at one time. ;)

To Omar Parkman, thank you for allowing me to use your image to bring Xavier Valentine to life! I appreciate you and wish you much success in all your endeavors.

Last but certainly not least, my family and friends. My son Noah, my husband Patrick, my mother Jessica. You guys are my squad, and I love you for life and hereafter!

This gift I have wouldn't be possible without my Lord and Savior manifesting it within me. Thank you, God, for everything. Your daughter, Steph.

To my readers, thank you so much for continuing to read my stories. It is my hope that each book gives you not only an escape but the joy and love jones I get while writing it. Shine bright Queens.

Chapter One

ISLAND HARBOUR, ANGUILLA

The sun hung high over the Caribbean island, threatening the beach goers with intimidating rays of heat. Underneath an umbrella, Corinne Thomas sat with a cocktail on a foldable table at her side. When she landed at Clayton J. Lloyd International Airport, Corinne made a beeline straight to the tiny beach that sat just east of Puerto Rico and The Virgin Islands. Corinne was no stranger to Anguilla. For the two years, she'd been a stewardess, having an extended layover there had become her time to take a load off.

During those intervals, Corinne would find the spot where she could relax and pretend to be someone else for the small window of time she was held up. In the beginning, Corinne changed her identity as a safety hazard. She couldn't go around telling strangers her government name.

It felt silly keeping up the pretense, but after it became common, Corinne stepped into her role quite nicely.

Corinne changed quickly in the airport restroom, grabbing a small tan beach chair and table. On her shoulder, she carried a large beach bag, and she didn't take the time to check into her hotel for the one night she would be there. Instead, Corinne led a trek to the sand and removed the dress she was wearing to reveal a mini metallic bikini. Auburn skin covered her body. Long arms and curvaceous thighs oozed through the thin straps and skimpy bottom as if it had been manufactured out of Willy Wonka's Chocolate Factory. Now she was stretched out on the lounge chair with a huge beach hat on top of her jet-black mane that hung straight down and trimmed the top of her shoulders.

Her mind was in another place as she brought the cocktail to her lips for a sip. More specifically, her mind was in Miami, Florida. It had been seven days since Hurricane Jasper flew through her hometown of Miami from the Florida Keys. The hurricane caught all of the residents by surprise since news reports stated earlier that the storm wouldn't hit until a week after it did.

At the time, Corinne had been homebound in Miami, along with her best friend Camilla Augustina and Camilla's parents. Because of the sudden storm, they all took immediate cover and for a long while none of them knew if they would make it out unharmed with the torrential winds and rain that slammed against the house's foundation. Only when Camilla's boyfriend and now fiancé Hunter Valentine emerged with his brother Xavier by his side to help them out did the foursome know the storm had passed.

A small smile cornered Corinne's lips as her mind conjured Xavier's mahogany brown skin that was distributed down his thick neck, muscular arms, and toned shoulders. Dark brown eyes stood out in her foresight, and his lids were draped as his orbs reached out to her with a piercing sting. His primed cut hair and neatly groomed beard complemented his hard mouth, and the spread of his lips shook up Corinne's core as they erupted into a sexy grin. Corinne took another sip of her cocktail, but it didn't slow down the daring thoughts of Xavier's dominant build and strapping physique. The first time she met him officially was on a blind double date that had gone so well Corinne had to stop herself from going back to his place and becoming the statistical one-night stand.

It was hard to do since Xavier was nothing but a complete gentleman, intelligent, and debonair. She learned quite a bit about him in the short span of time that they accompanied each other. Xavier was a sports agent; one of the best according to Google. Yeah, it was true, after that date, Corinne couldn't stop herself from putting his name in the search engine. What she'd found was an extended recap of things they'd discussed. Xavier graduated from Harvard with a bachelor's degree in sports and business management. After that he'd went on to get his master's, studying negotiation and marketing law.

His career excelled almost immediately when he negotiated a two-million-dollar contract for his first client, and since then his accolades had added on ten-fold. Pictures of Xavier at charity events surfaced, and there was always a handsome donation in the images. But another thing

Corinne took into account was the women. Every event seemed to bring forth a different woman. They ranged from different nationalities, but there was one who was recurring. The photo's caption said the woman was Nadine Benson, lady and daughter of Archduke Benjamin Forrest the third.

There weren't many things that intimidated Corinne, but she had to admit seeing the two in several photos made her wonder about the nature of their relationship. The entire evening of Corinne and Xavier's blind date, he did simple things that were easy for Corinne to notice since she'd only been with bums, and never experienced the full extent of a gentleman's moves. Pulling out chairs, holding open doors, ordering for her, paying for the check. Corinne took another sip as she continued to commemorate the evening. Simple things, yet noticeable. Besides that, their chemistry had held so much electricity that by the end of the night, Corinne felt completely fried. But again, Xavier's mannerisms were already shutting down rumors of him being a casualty to birds of a feather flock together. More straightforwardly, Xavier was a Valentine, the multi-million-aire family that had a significant hand in the flourishing of Chicago's economy.

They were born septuplets to powerhouse and media moguls Bridgette and Leslie Valentine. The men had been raised under the guidance of an influential father, and he'd taught his children the ropes, making sure they each went to ivy league schools and excelled at their careers. The men were at the top of their game, but with that celebrity came women, paparazzi, and tabloids. None of them had been immune to rumors in the media, not even Xavier. He,

Hunter, and Lance Valentine were usually the trio that caught the most heat because of their risky rendezvous and the interchangeable women on their arms.

It was the sole reason Corinne chose to ignore the strange chemistry between her and Xavier; it was clearly lust and nothing more, right? Corinne struggled to shift her thoughts, but each time she was brought back to the aftermath of Hurricane Jasper. Xavier and Hunter surprised the four of them at Camilla's family's bungalow. After pulling them out of the fallout shelter, Corinne couldn't hide the unmistakable adoration she experienced when Xavier pulled her into the comfort of his formidable chest.

"Are you all right?" His thick voice drummed.

Corinne swallowed, and her eyes fluttered while she wrestled to dismiss the sudden delight she felt.

"Yes," she said, meeting his gaze.

Xavier drove a thick finger down the side of her cheek and scrutinized her face to get a better look at her.

"Are you certain?

Corinne licked her lips, and Xavier's gaze dropped down to them.

"I'm sure," she said. "Thank you for coming down with Hunter. I'm sure you didn't appreciate flying through a storm."

Xavier smirked. "Not at first."

At Corinne's dubious expression, Xavier elaborated.

"My brother is in love, and when you're in love, you do strange things. I don't blame him, but at first, I thought he was crazy. Now I understand. It would've been me had I known my girl was caught in the crossfires of a cyclone. So, tell me, what are you doing in Florida? I was sure you would be halfway across the world by now.

"My flight was canceled. That happens sometimes."

"Hmmm, and you didn't think to call me when this storm hit?"

Corinne hesitated before responding. "And say what?"

Xavier stared at her for so long she thought he'd gone into a trance.

"I thought we were friends," he said.

"We are," Corinne added quickly.

"So why wouldn't you call your friend and tell him that you were caught in a storm?" Xavier continued before Corinne could respond. "You shouldn't have been here. What if the storm had been worse? We could've lost you."

Corinne stuttered. "W-we?" She said.

"Yeah…" he drawled. "Your parents and me."

Corinne had gone speechless after that. What exactly was he saying? She was almost afraid to ask. Afraid to wonder since his words felt more than friendly. She decided it was a part of his Casanova.

They were pulled from their musing when Hunter proposed to Camilla right then and there. Corinne was totally surprised along with Camilla's parents, but not Xavier. It was like he knew it was coming. Corinne peered over to look at Xavier, and he winked with a lazy smile hanging onto the edges of his masculine jaw. The day moved pretty fast after that, with them all packing up in the BMW Hunter purchased off the hands of a random stranger in his desperate attempt to get to Camilla. They drove back to

Hialeah Florida and boarded Xavier's private jet for Chicago. Since then, Corinne lodged with Camilla, but she may as well had been staying alone for all the company Camilla was. Corinne smiled again and took a final sip of her cocktail before putting the glass to the side and standing to her feet.

Her toes sank into the warm grains of sand, and she stretched her long limbs then removed her sunglasses and straw hat, sticking them both inside her beach bag near her chair. With a sway in her hips, Corinne padded out to the shoreline and entered the water just as it rushed her legs, making her quiver. Still, her reflections were with Xavier as she hosted silly notions of what-ifs and never-ending possibilities.

She dipped down into the waves and stretched out on her back, allowing her body to float on top of the rushing water. The chilly waves let her coast for a second before becoming disruptive and tossing her over. Corinne drifted with the sway in the seas, dipping under then swimming to the top for a reprieve. As she rose, she stood, and the sunlight shimmered off her metallic two-piece. She walked out of the waters like one of Charlie's Angels with her hair now plastered down her neck to her back. Rivulets ran down her skin as she approached her lounge chair to find someone occupying her space.

"Good evening, Angela."

Corinne smiled softly. "Good evening, Carlos," she said, greeting a friendly island native. "How did you know I was here?"

Carlos smiled. His ear-length silky hair waved as he

nodded. "I tour this island all of the time. Besides that, you have a routine."

Corinne smiled. "Do I?"

Carlos nodded again.

"Well, I was just getting ready to head to the hotel since the sun's setting."

"Oh, let me help you with your things."

Carlos moved toward her beach bag to lift it.

"No, no, Carlos, you're fine, it's just a bag, I can get it."

"What about your chair and table?"

"Those are easy to carry, too. They're simple to fold." Corinne made a show of folding up the beach chair without issue. "See." She tucked the small chair up under her arm and reached for her bag on Carlos's shoulder.

"Ms. Angela, you don't need to carry any of it. There's still the table," he stressed.

Corinne dropped the bag and folded the flimsy table then tucked it alongside the chair and lifted her bag.

"See," she said. "Thank you anyway, Carlos." Corinne patted him on the shoulder and strolled away. Without needing to look back, Corinne knew he was watching.

The first time she encountered Carlos, she was lying stretched out across a beach towel on her stomach. The tiny island only housed a little over a thousand residents, so it was easy for one to be noticed as a visitor. When Carlos stepped to her and introduced himself, Corinne didn't find it odd that he knew she was a stranger. Politely, she greeted him back and introduced herself as Angela. That was four months ago. Since then, whenever Corinne frequented the beach, Carlos would materialize out of nowhere. She would be relaxing one minute, then an enlarged shadow would be covering her the next. A few times he creeped her out appearing like that, but he seemed friendly enough, so she chose to ignore it.

Be that as it may, allowing Carlos to carry her items back to her hotel was out of the question. Though she'd warmed to him significantly since their initial meeting, Corinne was still not willing to go there. She didn't need Carlos getting the wrong idea. She was only interested in one person, but his rigorous work schedule sealed just about every hour in every day. Corinne continued her stroll to the hotel with thoughts of Xavier pending. The seven days between the last time Corinne had seen him were spent checking her line for text messages and waking up in the midnight hour to see if she'd missed a call. To her pleasure, there would be a single sentence in her text window around the same time every night.

Thinking of you.

Corinne's nerves tickled her system, and she recognized that she was in like with Xavier. Not only that, but she thought, just maybe, he was in like with her, too. He was busier than the president, so taking the time to send that text at what Corinne assumed was the end of his day made her warm inside. Corinne sighed, entering the hotel and taking the elevator to her floor. As she passed each level, she wondered what Xavier was up to, and if he was thinking of her at that moment, too.

Chapter Two

CHICAGO, ILLINOIS

*X*avier reached for his undershirt and pulled it over his massive shoulders then tossed it in a clothing bin he passed on the way to the master bathroom. It was almost midnight, and negotiations with this latest contract had stalled for longer than he liked. However, after going back and forth through several rounds, Xavier came out the victor. His negotiation skills were tough and no-nonsense. Since he'd been in the business, league representatives cringed after finding out he was the agent, knowing whatever Xavier went for he usually retained. It had been a rough couple of days, but Xavier was determined to seal the deal on this contract today, and so he did. Inside the bathroom, Xavier bypassed the clawfoot tub in favor of the glass shower stall and adjusted the water's temperature to his pleasure.

He didn't waste time getting in; Xavier was in need of

the tranquility he found in the steamy bath. He soaked for more than an hour, letting the rainfall needle his muscles and massage his shoulders. With his head under the spray, Xavier closed his eyes, and images of the only person he'd thought of for the past week resurfaced, Corinne Thomas. When he met her, Xavier wasn't prepared for the flourish of emotions that gripped him. When he reasoned why they were there, Xavier alleged it must've been his intense attraction to her. Corinne was a beautiful woman with her daring almond-shaped eyes and risqué appearance. He remembered her laugh, dark and sultry. It had gripped his heart a couple of times, and Xavier made an effort to shake it off repeatedly. But when Corinne was caught in the pathway of Hurricane Jasper, Xavier found a new reason to want her. It wasn't something that he searched for purposefully, but rather an odd necessity to keep her close.

With his mind craving constant thoughts of her, Xavier left his bathroom with a towel wrapped haphazardly around his waist. In the bedroom, he strolled to his closet and removed a tailored Armani suit he would wear the next day.

"Corinne..." he mused, his thoughts taking him on a trip to his cell phone. Retrieving the device, he strolled through his contacts and tapped her icon to send a message. He was halfway through typing, *Thinking of You,* when he erased the words and opted for a phone call. Now standing idly by his nightstand, Xavier waited for her to answer, but it was late, and it appeared his call would go to voicemail. As he cleared his throat to leave his message, the ringing in his ear stopped, and her dark throaty voice cruised through the line.

"Hello…"

Xavier closed his eyes and mentally calmed the beat of his heart.

"Did I catch you at a bad time," his deep voice strummed.

There was movement on the other end of the line.

"Xavier?"

"Were you expecting someone else?"

More movement on the other end.

"No, I actually wasn't expecting anyone but especially not you." Corinne paused then moved forward with her explanation. "You know, with you being the head of secret service and all."

A smile peppered across his lips, and a grizzly chuckle coursed from his throat.

"Aren't you the comic of the hour," he said, his voice also dark and daring.

"I thought it was funny," she joked.

Xavier nodded. "It was a good one." A long pause threaded their connection. "I've missed you."

On the other end, Corinne clutched the phone with a tight fist. Her pulse accelerated, and a warm coat of delight poured over her.

"I've," she paused, "missed you, too."

"Have you?"

Corinne melted into the comfort of the hotel covers. "I have."

"Prove it," he said.

Corinne gawked. "How can I do that?"

"Meet me halfway between where you are and where I am, right now."

Corinne's thoughts tangled, and a spiraling thrill of energy wrapped around her skin. "Unfortunately, that's impossible," she said.

"I have no recollection of the word impossible. Tell me where you are, and I'll show you."

Corinne's heart raced at an all-time high. His promise made her pull from the covers and race to the bathroom to check her overall appearance. There was a bonnet on her head. A colorful one at that. The knee length button down silk nightgown was oversized, but Corinne could only sleep in clothes double her size for the comfort and loose fit of them. Her reflex told her to lose the bonnet and the shirt and put on something sexy, but her common sense said there was no way he could get to her tonight, unless he was a magician.

"Xavier, that's sweet, but I'm in Anguilla. We are stuck on a layover until morning."

"We?" he asked.

"I mean, the crew and me."

"I see."

She heard the disappointment in his tone.

"Where is your next destination?" he asked.

"Um..." she murmured, "For the next layover, Salt Lake City."

"Utah?"

She chuckled. "Yeah, sounds like fun, huh?"

"Hmmm, I can think of a thing or two to get into if you're game."

Corinne opened her mouth then thought about her words and licked her lips. She didn't want to sound overtly excited. Besides, this was Xavier Valentine we were talking about. Even with their instant chemistry and the possibility of a romance brewing, it didn't mean it was actually so.

"Do you have the free time? I thought you were busy with—"

"Corinne..."

His thunderous voice drug out her name, sending an impetuous shiver over her skin.

"I'll always be busy with impending deals on the horizon, but I make time for what's important."

"And seeing me in Salt Lake City is important?"

"Seeing you is important. The place, time, or event is a non-factor."

Corinne's eyes enlarged with surprise, and she took a hand to her neck and drove it down her chest.

"Why?" she asked.

On the other end of the phone, Xavier had moved from his bedside to the entrance of his master quarters. Leaning a shoulder into the doorjamb, he licked his lips and took a sturdy hand down his beard, deciding to tell her what he'd been thinking the last couple of days.

"Honestly, Corinne, I hadn't been on a date for years before our blind date. And I'm talking about a real date, where I'm interested in the other person I'm with." He paused and added, "Most women that have been spotted in the media with me were merely for the show of having a companion. When I agreed to the blind date, it was to get out of my normal routine of non-stop exertion. But you..."

Corinne swallowed and kept still as she waited for him to finish that train of thought.

"I never expected to meet someone like you. Beauty aside, your intelligence on the state of our country, the passion you spoke with, and the spiciness in your retorts when I challenged you left me, thirsting."

A ripple of heat in a somersault of chills sprinkled down Corinne's skin. She remembered that conversation all too well because Xavier had ruffled her with his rhetoric about the presidency being on the right road to recovering our nation. Several times, she'd been ready to get up and walk out on him, and usually she would have had it been some other bum talking through an ignorant lens, but this was Xavier Valentine. He wasn't ignorant nor a bum, and with the voice he had, Corinne needed him to know how wrong he was and why.

"You took me on headstrong, and no one's ever done that before."

Corinne's brows rose. "Really?"

"Really."

"So, you're one of those celebrities that everyone just agrees with and tells you what you want to hear?"

Xavier chuckled. "I'd hardly qualify as a celebrity," he said.

"If you believe that, then I may have to go toe to toe with you again about how wrong you are."

His chuckle became dangerously delicious as it beat through the phone and scorched her ear.

"I love that about you, too."

"What's that?"

Now Corinne's voice held that dark throaty sound that Xavier grew to cherish every time he had the honor of hearing it.

"Your sense of humor. I feel like I could talk to you about anything, and whether we agreed or not, it would be a nourishing debate." He paused, and Corinne blushed unaware of how to respond.

"So, what do you say, Corinne, meet me in Salt Lake City?"

Corinne's smile lifted her face. How could she refuse his request?

"It's going to take me about ten hours to get there, maybe longer depending on connecting flights. I won't have the details of our stops until I board tomorrow."

"Is that a yes?" he asked, making her slap her forehead.

Xavier didn't fair well with excuses, so after she was finished tossing that thought around, the only thing he needed to know was if she would welcome him should he come.

"Okay," she acquiesced. "I'll meet you in Salt Lake City."

Chapter Three

KINSHIP AIRLINES

The next day

"*Ladies and gentlemen, we have landed at Northwest Arkansas Regional Airport. The local time is seven-thirty p.m., and the temperature is seventy-six degrees. For your security, please make sure your seats are back and remain seated with your belts firmly fastened.*

When the captain turns off the fasten your seat belt sign, we will be stationed at the gateway. This would be the optimum time to use your cellular devices if the need occurs.

Be sure to examine your area compartments for additional luggage, and please use caution when opening the overhead bins. If you're headed to Salt Lake City, Utah, you have the option of exiting the aircraft to take care of any needs you may have or you're welcome to stay on board. Flight 59B will be re-boarding again in one hour. On behalf of Kinship Airlines, I'd like to thank you for flying with us."

Corinne placed the intercom's receiver back on the wall and waited patiently for the fasten your seat belt sign to dim. When it did, she unbuckled her safety strap and made her way along with two other stewardesses to the main cabin. She helped direct the crowd to the exit while thanking them for flying Kinship Airlines. There was a smile on her face and cheer in her eyes, and although it was perfect for her job description, the excitement she felt had nothing to do with the airlines or the passengers.

Hearing Xavier tell her last night that she was important to him in so many words thrilled and scared her to death. Apparently, Xavier was fond of her, and while Corinne would've like to believe she already knew this, she wasn't one to assume. Their blind date had been great, their phone conversations albeit light always ended to her satisfaction. Him showing up with Hunter to rescue her like a damsel in distress did add a level of delight to their communications, but to outright say she was important was next level. As the last passenger exited so did Corinne, deciding to stretch her legs, use the ladies' room, and grab a quick bite to eat.

She mused as she went about her tasks, wondering what Xavier had in mind when they arrived in Utah. Corinne smirked. She knew he was a traveler, but Corinne could hardly imagine him in Salt Lake City. When Corinne thought of Xavier, she imagined glamour and big city lights. When she thought of Salt Lake City, thoughts of the Mormon church and Kentucky Fried Chicken came to mind, mostly because the city was known for being the headquarters of The Church of Jesus Christ of Latter-day Saints and the original home of KFC.

Still, out of all of the traveling Corinne had done, she'd never felt so charmed to make it to a destination. Corinne left the bathroom and headed for the sink. She washed her hands and checked her appearance then readjusted the uniformed shirt that represented her as an employee of Kinship Airlines. Drying her hands, Corinne continued to muse, then left the restroom for food. After thirty minutes, Corinne made her way back to the aircraft where she boarded and headed to the break room. She was still transfixed in thought when a familiar baritone voice reached out to touch her skin.

"Good evening, mademoiselle."

Corinne's steps halted, and she twirled to the side. Surprise registered on her face as her eyes lit up, and her mouth parted slightly. Xavier Valentine seemed to get more attractive every time she saw him if that was even remotely possible. He was casually dressed, wearing an all-white premium-fitted crewneck T-shirt that kissed the brawniness in his muscles and stretched over his immense chest. The pullover rode down his chiseled abdomen into a pair of denim jeans that kissed his robust thighs before extending down to a fresh white pair of classic Reeboks. Around his neck a simple gold herringbone necklace draped; in his ears small diamond studs cast a soft sparkle. But behind all of that, Xavier's mahogany skin lured her, looking so sweet Corinne caught an instant toothache. His gaze brimmed, partially suspended as he took in her almond-shaped eyes, full lips, and smooth brown skin. Her uniformed attire may as well have been absent for all the good it was doing. Xavier could see straight through the fabric, and his imagination tortured him with thoughts of what she could look like underneath.

"Xavier, how did you…?"

A smirk tugged his lips, and he withdrew his hands from his pockets as he closed the distance between them.

"Sometimes, I can be an impatient man," he admitted, gazing down into her eyes. Hypnotized, Corinne stared back as his lips moved and his extended beard waved across her chin, tickling her skin. Reacting to the sensation, a smile cruised across her lips. "And I couldn't wait," he lifted two fingers to her chin and pulled her in, "to do this."

His glorious lips sank into hers and spread Corinne's mouth to allow his tongue a place to rest. The moan came from the depths of her soul, and Corinne lifted feeling light as a feather on her toes. As his lips devoured her slowly, Corinne sank into the closeness of his chest with her hands sliding up his muscle-toned barricade. Her body's heat index was aflame, but another sheath of warmth shrouded her when his arms glided around her waist and covered her back. She was lost, in a space and time where only Xavier could reach her. Their tongues slipping and sliding, then sucking as they both tasted the inner recesses of their apertures. A thumping in the seat of her panties made Corinne's entire nervous system come to life, and she was discreetly aware of the painful pushing against Xavier's zipper.

"Ahem."

Someone cleared their throat, and it severed the spellbinding allure that had fallen over Corinne. She snapped her head back, and their lips parted on a mouthwatering smack. However, Corinne didn't glance to the newcomer right away; instead, she stared up at Xavier with wonder and a heartwarming appreciation. His gaze lingered on her mouth before returning to meet her eyes and there, he detained her.

"We're boarding," the female voice came. Corinne recognized the voice as Monica's, another stewardess on board.

Pulling herself with significant force to acknowledge Monica was more difficult than anything. But when she did, Corinne nodded and stepped slightly away from Xavier.

"Thank you," Corinne said to Monica.

Monica lingered with a huge grin and a conspiratorial wink in her eye. Monica moved off, going to the main cabin to welcome passengers on flight 59B. Corinne cleared her throat.

"Maybe you should have a seat," she whispered, still trying to reclaim her voice. "It looks like we'll be taking off soon."

"Is it possible for you to share a seat with me?" he asked.

"Um, no, I don't think so."

"You don't think?"

"That's never been a request before, but we have safety rules in place that would most likely prevent it."

"I see."

Xavier slipped his hands back into his pockets, needing to keep them hidden so not to grab Corinne again and haul her into his arms.

"I have another request," he said.

"Okay," she said, waiting.

"I'd like to change my seat. I'll pay extra if it's needed."

Corinne swept her eye around the cabin.

"Where would you like to sit?"

"Near you," he said.

Corinne smirked then giggled, dropping her head in a sway then looking back at him. "You never give up, do you?"

"You're just noticing that?"

Corinne giggled again. "I sit in the corner seat up ahead." She pointed to the area the stewardess sat. "The closest you could get would be this window seat, and it wouldn't be extra."

"All right then." Xavier retrieved a suitcase she hadn't noticed before and followed behind Corinne to the seat in question. He sat down and got comfortable, stretching his long legs to relax.

"Would you like anything, Mr. Valentine?" He looked at her with a mischievous grin, and Corinne added, "Anything from the airline's menu?" She was tickled when his delight turned into a frown.

"Only from the menu?"

"For now," she said.

Xavier smiled wide. "Then no, I'm good," he added, "for now."

———

IT WAS THE MOST INTENSE FLIGHT CORINNE HAD ENDURED thus far. After making her rounds to check on each passenger, Corinne returned to the stewardess seat and crossed her legs. The plane had been airborne for an hour, and Xavier was fast asleep. Corinne knew he must've been exhausted, but he refused to rest like a normal human being and recharge. She surmised he was a machine, driven by adrenaline and the basic key nutrition that would keep him invigorated. Corinne drove a lackadaisical eye over Xavier. With his head inclined against the seat, and his eyes drawn to a close, she drew a blueprint of the schematics of his charming face, leaving no detail excluded. It held a soft edge in his sleep, and his chest pushed and pulled quietly as he breathed. Her eyes rode down the colossal mastery of his muscular arms that were propped on the rests of the chair at the elbows. In his lap, Xavier's hands gathered, and his fingers linked to rest against his brown leather Saint Laurent belt.

Corinne's tongue tasted the corners of her mouth as she continued to peruse him, and his toned thighs made the jeans, not the other way around. At his feet his ankles were crossed, and the Reeboks were so crisp they appeared as if he'd just pulled them from the box. Corinne had never felt so turned on by a man resting peacefully in his slumber, and for a long minute, she contemplated what it must be like to be the leading lady in his life. Could she withstand the lens they would surely be under once word spread that they were dating? Could she compare to the women he'd dated previously, models, actresses, and a royalty?

Corinne drifted off in such a daze that she didn't notice when Xavier's eyes fluttered open, and his lids hovered, just slightly taking in her full beauty. He watched her watching him without Corinne's awareness. He wondered what was going on in that pretty little head of hers as his gaze journeyed over her face. The uniform she wore didn't own her, and although it was professional, her curves would not be hidden. Corinne sat posed with a silky brown leg crossed over the other. The fullness in her thighs traveled to her hips, and they curved like the stroke of a painter's brush. Xavier's skin tingled with a sulfuric heat, instantly, like he'd been smacked with it. Her beauty was unparalleled to anyone he'd ever laid eyes on, but what stirred him the most was her unmoving attitude, and he wanted to know her inside and out.

"What's on your mind, beautiful?"

Corinne's daze was snagged when his profound voice scurried over her skin. She squirmed in her seat, and her eyes met his thick, penetrating stare.

"Oh, nothing," she said. "I didn't realize you were awake."

Xavier didn't respond immediately, needing to let her risqué voice filter the drum in his ear.

"You're not being honest with me," he said. "Why?"

Stirred, Corinne's brows rose before ruffling in a frown.

"I wasn't trying to be untruthful, I just." She sighed. "I was just thinking about how tired you must be after all the work you do and wondering why you would trade your rest to be here," she added, "with me."

Xavier hung on to her gaze for another long moment, then the corner of his lips curved. "But you know why."

Corinne cleared her throat and shifted again in her seat. "I still wonder." She decided to change the subject to something that wouldn't make her nervous system a wreck. "So, we'll be in Utah in about thirty minutes. You've slept most of the trip. Can I get you anything?"

Xavier glanced toward the window but could only see dark clouds. When he pulled his attention back, he pulled his legs in and lifted himself properly in the seat.

"I could use a bottle of water."

Corinne moved quickly, happy to get him the cold water he needed. She needed a cold shower with the way her body continued to flame. How would she be able to endure a day with him, never mind a night? There was a quick trot in her footing as she dashed into the kitchen and rumbled inside the refrigerator. While getting his water, Corinne grabbed her one, too. She hadn't thought this thing through. Yes, she wanted to spend some time with him, but at night? Doing what?

"Shit," she cursed, worried that she'd given Xavier the wrong impression. He thought she was important, he'd said as much, and she was holding on to that sentiment. It helped her not feel like she was leading him on with this trip he'd taken to get to her. But what if he wanted sex when they made it to their destination? *As if you don't want it.* She shushed her inner thoughts. That was beside the point, she mused. If she were being realistic, she and Xavier had been communicating for about three weeks now. It wasn't necessarily normal everyday communications, but the text messages count. Didn't they? Corinne almost moaned with frustration. Truthfully, she wanted him, and she couldn't deny that she'd imagined all the ways that he could please her sexually.

But what if that was his endgame? What if he told all

the women he bedded that they were important? She didn't want to be his fool, and Corinne was still feeling him out. As she stood frozen with the aircraft's refrigerator door open, a soft click behind her pulled her attention. She glanced over her shoulder and found Xavier standing a mere foot behind her. He mounted there, hosing her down with a stentorious inspection. A ripple coursed down her flesh, and the water bottles in her hands were squeezed tightly as her gut constricted.

She went into defense mode immediately. "Xavier, you can't be back here," she blubbered quickly. "I could get in trouble if anyone saw you."

He took a step toward her. "If that happens, I'll have a talk with the pilot," he said.

Corinne gawked then closed her mouth. "And say what?"

Xavier shrugged. "I'll donate to the charity of his choice for keeping it our secret."

A throaty but vibrant laugh ballooned from Corinne. "You're serious."

"Do I make you nervous, Corinne?"

His question stumped her, and while she thought about telling him the truth or being vague with her response, Xavier moved closer to her.

"No," she lied, "why would you ask that?"

"No?"

He knew she was lying, and instead of repeating the fib, Corinne simply shook her head but sealed her lips just as he made it into her personal space.

"Your body language says something different, sweetheart." With his left index finger, he drove a line down her arm. "You're holding on to those bottles mighty tightly."

Just as he mentioned it, the tops on the bottles popped from the death squeeze she had. Corinne jumped, and a shriek slipped from her mouth. Embarrassed, Corinne tried to step around him, but he locked her between his massive frame and the open refrigerator. Corinne was relieved about one thing, at least the coolness from the icebox helped calm her raging hormones. She pushed out a breath.

"Okay, yes," she said, going for the truth this time. "You do make me nervous."

A grin slipped across his mouth. "Why?"

Corinne sighed heavily again. "I don't know maybe because I like you, but I'm still not sure about your intentions with me."

That paused his questioning, and he straightened from the hovering he was doing. "I understand," he said. "Do you think I'm an honest man, Corinne?"

"I—"

His gaze bore into her, letting her know that she should continue down this path of truth.

Corinne squeezed out a breath. "I want to believe you are. In business, I don't doubt it, but in your personal, or dating life, I'm not sure who you are yet."

Xavier nodded. "That's fair enough."

Corinne was relieved to hear that.

"Will you give me the chance to show you who I am before you judge me?"

That just made Corinne feel like an ass. She had, after all, judged him immediately.

"I'm sorry, Xavier, I never meant to question your integrity."

"It's quite all right. You have every reason to. Like you said, you're still getting to know me, so it's normal for you to feel this way. But, will you give me the chance to show you who I am and possibly who I can become to you?"

Corinne swallowed hard, and her body's nerves went crazy. She leaned into him without realizing it as if she were pulled magnetically forward. Her short approach caused Xavier to react with one arm slipping around her waist and the other gliding up her neck to grip the back of her head.

"And another thing," his thick voice ticked. "If you get this close to me, I won't stop myself from tasting you. Here is some of my honesty. I'm attracted to you, Corinne, thoroughly. And I can tell that you're attracted to me." His hand slipped up her waist and combed over her arm, shoulder, and closed in on the other side of her neck. He pulled her so close their lips were separated by a wisp of air. "So I won't regret kissing you, and I won't regret touching you. And unless you tell me you don't want me to, I will." He waited for her to object, giving her optimal time to consider his words. When she didn't, he took her lips to his with a slow delicate tasting of her mouth. Corinne's entire body shuddered, and the water bottles slipped from her hands and hit the floor.

It didn't disturb them. In fact, Corinne's arms glided around his toned waist and her acceptance of his kiss caused him to suck her in wholly.

"Mmmm," she moaned, as her pussy thumped, completely taken by him. Her body writhed as the energy around them struck her like a flash of lightning, and she liquified into his embrace.

Bing! "Good evening, ladies and gentlemen, this is your captain speaking. I hope you've enjoyed your flight on board Kinship Airlines. As we are approaching Salt Lake City International Airport, please be sure that your seat belts are securely fastened. Flight attendants, prepare for landing please. Cabin crew, please take your seats."

Heeding the captain's request, Xavier pulled from their erotic kiss but not before placing a few down Corinne's chin and an animalistic bite at the edge of her jaw.

"We should probably—"

"Yeah," Corinne interrupted, still dazed and unsure her legs were steady enough to move.

Xavier kissed her cheek one last time then stepped to her side and slipped his hand in hers.

"Shall we?"

Chapter Four

$\mathcal{I}$t was amazing how calm her spirit was now that they were in the lobby of the Courtyard by Marriott Hotel. As Corinne thought about it, Xavier's candor on the plane seemed to put her worries temporarily to rest, but she was still reeling from the ramifications of that kiss.

"Thank you," Xavier said, taking the key to their rooms off the receptionist's hands. He turned to Corinne and slipped his palm down her back, letting it rest in the curve of her spine. "Are you ready?" he asked.

Corinne nodded with a smile, and they both moved toward the elevators. With the press of a button, the doors dinged, and Xavier and Corinne strolled inside. Corinne turned toward the doors, and Xavier turned to her.

"For you," he said, handing her a room key.

Corinne took the key out of his hand, perplexed.

"You're room 223, I'm 225," he said.

"Oh."

Why did she feel slightly disappointed that they would be in separate quarters? Feeling indifferent and somewhat confused by her indecision, Corinne smiled curtly and responded, "Thank you."

"You're welcome."

The elevator reached its floor, and the doors opened.

"This is us," Xavier said.

They exited and strolled side by side in silence down the hall. When they reached Corinne's room, Xavier removed the key from her fingers and inserted it into the door. The green light illuminated, and he returned the key to her palm and opened it, holding it for her to enter.

"Since we only have a half a day with each other tomorrow, I was hoping you would have dinner with me tonight."

Corinne tilted her head with a smirk. "Of course, Xavier. You came all this way just to keep me company on a layover. I think I can spend some time with you over food." She grinned. "Besides, I'd love to."

Xavier's heart warmed, and he reached for her fingers and linked them with his. Drawing her to him, Xavier placed a tender kiss on one temple than the other. Then a soft kiss on the tip of her nose.

Corinne giggled. "Okay, that tickles."

"Does it?"

"Yeah," she said with her face turned up to him and her mouth holding a wide beam of a smile.

"What about this?" he said, sinking his mouth into hers. Corinne inhaled the breath he released. Her eyes closed, and a riveting bolt attacked her senses. She wanted to linger there and indulge in the pull of his lips and the exploration of his tongue, but just as quickly as the kiss began, Xavier ended it, withdrawing from her as if it was in his best interest to do so.

"Wait," Corinne said. It was almost as if someone else had spoken it, making Corinne surprised by her own request. She reopened her eyes to find Xavier's bristling gaze pinned on her. Corinne swallowed. "More," she said. It came out like a faint whisper.

"Corinne…"

"I want more," she said, rejecting his opposition.

The suitcase in his hand dropped and in synchronization they both went at each other. Corinne jumped into his arms, and Xavier lifted her with a handful of her ass. Her legs entwined around his waist, and their mouths crashed against one another in an urgent haste to transform into one. Heat ballooned from their toes and met up with another trail of fire that tracked from the crown of their heads. It gathered in the center of their joining, and a ragged moan slipped from Corinne at the feel of his extended erection prodding against the seat of her panties.

"Mmmm," she moaned.

Xavier pulled his mouth from hers but only to travel down her chin and place deep saturating kisses underneath her neck in a stalk down her throat.

"Oh… Xavier, take me inside."

In the frame of the doorway, their breathing labored, and Xavier's kisses lightened, then he pulled his gaze to hers. He looked like a bull with his nostrils flaring and his teeth partially bared. There was an inner fight going on inside of him; Corinne could see it and wondered what it meant. Did he want her? Or was he worried about her only wanting sex. Corinne half-rolled her eyes at that last thought. Of course, he wasn't worried about that. She was losing her mind. Without a word, Xavier moved inside her room with long strides to the king size bed. He paused again, his mind moving so fast Corinne could practically see his thoughts in a twirl.

"What is it?" She asked, curiously interested. With her arms around his neck, she tightened her thighs and lifted to rotate her pelvis against his. He needed to take advantage and stat while she still had the courage.

Xavier groaned like a wounded animal then bit down on his teeth, and Corinne leaned in to place heated kisses on the pillar of his throat. When he spoke, his voice was gruff and profound.

"We should wait," he said.

Corinne paused and slowly she pulled back to stare at him. Xavier wanted her to trust him fully, and he knew that at that moment, she didn't. As much as he would like to rip her clothes to shreds and bury himself in the deepest part of her, he also wanted more; that he was sure of. Corinne was interested in his intentions, and he planned to show her, even if his dick didn't approve.

Corinne searched his face. "Um."

"Listen," he took his mouth to her nose and kissed it, "when you give yourself to me, I want you to be one hundred percent sure that you trust me to take care of you. I want you to know who I am and feel sure about the decision you're making."

Corinne understood, and she respected Xavier for that, but it didn't make her want to cry any less. She was literally suspended on the ridge of his solid erection. Her mind agreed with Xavier, it was the right thing to do, but her body said something else entirely. Corinne tried to climb out of his arms, and his massive dick punctured her belly as she slid down his body on the way to her feet. The whimper that left her mouth was her body's way of mourning the pleasure it was being denied, and Corinne made sure to coach herself into staying on track. Xavier helped her gain her balance. She didn't even know what to say. Xavier had rendered her speechless.

"I'm going to freshen up and will return within the hour." He held a long lingering eye on Corinne. She smiled up at him and nodded. "Are you okay?"

He wanted her to know she could trust him, but not at the expense of her thinking he didn't want her.

"I'm fine. I need to freshen up, too."

He ran a hand down her shoulder and nodded. "Be back in a minute." He turned and strolled across the room, and Corinne decided not to watch him leave. When the door clicked, she let out a dragging exhale and fell back on the bed. Looking at the ceiling, Corinne remembered the conversation she and her best friend Camilla had when Camilla and her now fiancé had just spent a blissful night together.

Camilla was in a state of constant euphoria, and Corinne was bubbling beside her. Corinne remembered it so well because that's how she felt now, except they hadn't spent a night with each other, and she hoped she hadn't made a complete fool of herself. One thing was for sure, Xavier was doing a good job showing his sincerity. Corinne didn't know any man who could've turned down all that ass she'd just put on him. Corinne giggled and grabbed a pillow and covered her face. She needed to talk this out and that made her pull to a sit and reach for her tote.

Inside, she fished for her phone then found Camilla's number and hit send. After two rings, Camilla answered the phone.

"Well hello, hello," Camilla said.

"Hey, girl, are you busy?"

"Not at the moment. What's up, where are you now?"

"Salt Lake City."

"Poor thing, you must be bored out of your mind."

"Actually, I'm not."

Camilla became intrigued. "Do tell."

"I'm on another twenty-four-hour layover and I'm not alone."

"I'm listening."

"Xavier," Corinne said.

Corinne heard a shuffle through the phone then Camilla's voice came back through a bit louder this time.

"Okay, give me all the juice," she said.

Corinne laughed. "What were you doing before?"

"Wrapped up with Hunter, what do you think?"

Corinne laughed again. Since Camilla and Hunter had gotten engaged, they'd been nearly inseparable.

"Now, I don't feel so bad about not being there with

your pregnant ass," Corinne said. "You're never home anyway."

"Hmmm, I can't apologize, girl. Why be at home when I can be with my babe?"

Corinne smiled brightly.

"Anyway, I'm in the kitchen now going through the fridge so talk fast before I eat everything in here."

Corinne laughed again. "Well you're eating for two now, so you're entitled to double stuff."

"Girl, please, then I'll have double the hips, and you know I can't have that."

"As if Hunter would mind."

Camilla smirked. "He wouldn't, but that is beside the point. Now, tell me what's going on. How did you and Xavier end up in Salt Lake City together?"

Corinne sighed. "I was in Anguilla, and we were on the phone. He asked me to meet him halfway between where we both were, but I couldn't. Long story short, I told him Salt Lake City was my next move, and he said he'd meet me there. But instead of him meeting me there, he met me at the connecting flight stop. I have no idea how he found out where the plane would be."

"All it takes really is a simple search with the airlines. You could find out where each plane is stopping."

"That's not something you can just search," Corinne said. "I mean it is, but it could take you forever to find the specific plane, where it is now, where it's landing, connecting flights, all of that. For goodness' sake I'm not a regular passenger you can search for. I'm an employee. So to find out which plane I was on had to have been a miracle. I mean who has time for that?"

"Apparently, he does. Have you put it on him yet? I know sometimes you can be a little scandalous," she joked.

Aghast, Corinne planted her hand against her hip. "No, you didn't," she said, listening to Camilla teeter over in laughter. "For your information…" Corinne paused. "Hell yeah, I did," she admitted.

This time it was Camilla who gasped so hard it almost knocked the wind out of her. "Are you serious!?"

Corinne laughed then snorted. "You sound so appalled," she said, continuing her laugh.

"That's because I was just joking!"

"Un huh, looks like I got the last laugh."

"Corinne!"

Corinne fell over laughing so hard she had to hold her stomach.

"Corinne!" Camilla yelled again.

Catching her breath, Corinne propped herself up on an elbow, a smile still covering her face. "So, what if we had sex, why is that a bad thing?" Corinne said, keeping up her shenanigans.

"It's not that it's a bad thing," Camilla said, unsure. "I just, well, I guess I didn't expect to hear that you guys hopped in the sack so soon. I thought you were going for the long ride with him, not just the ol' hop in the sack routine."

"Were you not the one that just called me scandalous?"

"I was only kidding!"

Corinne chuckled. "I was, too," she admitted.

"What?" Camilla said, now leaning a hand into her hip.

"Xavier and I have not slept together. Yet," she added.

Camilla let out a staunch breath and hustled across the kitchen to the basket of fruit. There, she grabbed a banana, peeled it quickly, then took a big bite of the sweet treat.

"Girl," Camilla said with a mouth full of banana, "you've made me hungry with this nonsense."

Corinne's laughter picked back up; she could tell by the muffled tone of Camilla's voice that she was stuffing her face. Just then Corinne's line beeped and she pulled the device from her ear to glance at the screen. Unknown number. Corinne rolled her eyes. She never understood why someone would seek another person out but restrict access to their digits. If you didn't want the receiver to know it was you, just don't call was her motto.

"Is that why you called me, to get me all riled up late at night?"

"Late? It's ten-thirty."

"That's the normal time most families get in the bed. Anyway, I take that as a yes since you didn't answer my question."

"No, you're wrong. I called you because I needed to get this off my chest." Corinne pulled herself to a sit and folded her legs underneath each other. "I like him."

Camilla waited for her to go on, but Corinne didn't.

"Is that all, I think we both already knew this."

"No, you don't understand. I like him a lot. It's unnatural, like some sort of weird sorcery."

Now Camilla was laughing.

"What's so funny?"

"Do you remember when you said having a conversation

with an intelligent brother will make you come in seconds without even being touched?"

"Yeah."

"Well, it sounds like you're getting a taste of what I've been experiencing this entire time." Camilla lowered her tone so that she wasn't whispering, but her vocals transformed into a deep sultry purr. "You're dating a Valentine. I have no doubt that Xavier is just as charming as Hunter." Camilla paused. "Well, almost," she decided.

"I have a confession."

"I'm listening."

"I almost jumped his bones. No, no, I did jump his bones. He was the one that stopped us. I've got to admit, I don't feel bad about it."

"Yeah, I won't shame you. I fed Hunter breakfast with my fingers when we first met."

Corinne's mouth dropped, and by her silence, Camilla knew Corinne's mouth was stuck.

"Sure did. We had known each other," Camilla shrugged. "Thirty minutes perhaps." She sighed. "Best damn breakfast I ever had."

Corinne fell over again in a howl. "Why am I just now hearing about this?!"

"Girl, because I couldn't get the man off my mind. You're right, it's sorcery."

The two friends laughed harder and agreed on one thing: getting mixed up with a Valentine was like being under a captivating spell.

"This can't be healthy," Corinne said.

"Honey, speak for yourself. There isn't a thing anyone could do or say that would make me think twice."

Corinne was nodding. "We're getting ready to have dinner, and yes, I know it's late, but we've just been able to get settled. Honestly, I think he's offering for my benefit. The man is not human the way he goes, goes, goes."

"That's the drive in him. Don't worry, if you guys are hitting it off the way I think you might, you will come second to nothing."

Corinne absorbed her friend's assessment and at the same time wrestled with nervousness.

"Anyway, you should get ready for your late-night dinner, and I'm going back to bed."

"Bye, honey, talk to you sometime soon."

"Um, tomorrow, I want the deets."

Corinne chuckled. "Okay."

"Good night."

They disconnected the line, and Corinne removed herself from the bed. She grabbed her tote and shuffled around inside, grabbing her oils and perfumes and a comfortable summer dress. With her other hand, she reached in and removed her charger port then found a socket on the wall. As she plugged her smartphone up, Corinne noted the time. Xavier said he would be back within the hour. Even though she probably didn't have time, Corinne's freshening up consisted of a ten-minute shower that would help her wash off the day.

It turned out to be fifteen minutes, but that was fine since Xavier had yet to knock on her door. Corinne drifted from the bathroom to the bedroom while she blot-dried her skin with a towel. She headed to her bag and pulled lotions and mixed them with her oil essentials then proceeded to apply a perfect shine to her skin. Corinne was lost in thought when she heard a familiar voice that seemed oddly close to her. She paused the stroke against her legs and listened.

"Draft up the official email." His voice was muffled. Corinne abandoned what she was doing to follow the voice. "You don't need me for this. If they come back with a counteroffer, recounter with the same number."

Corinne paused when she came to a wooden door, and there she could hear Xavier's voice clearly. "Adjoining rooms?" she said to herself. A curve took shape at the corner of her lips, and she traveled back across the room to what she was doing. Quickly dressing, that small feeling of rejection she felt earlier was gone now. If Xavier had gotten adjoining rooms, it must've been because he wanted to be close to her. Corinne swept her shoulder length hair to the side.

She wouldn't wait for him to come for her; this time, she was going to him.

Chapter Five

hen Xavier swung open the door, his cell phone was still pressed against his ear, but his forward thought was instantly filched. His gaze poured over Corinne's comfortable look, and although it was a simple summer dress, her four-inch heels and the way the fabric lay against her body made his dick excruciatingly hard pronto.

"Handle it," he said into the receiver, ending the call straight away. "Hey," he said to her.

"Hey," she responded, unable to hide a blush. "Are you busy, or can I come in?"

Xavier blinked back from his trance and quickly moved to the side. "Of course. No, I'm not busy."

Corinne stepped inside, giving Xavier a peek at the back of her dress. The thin material hung off her shoulders and covered her back to rest comfortably on the curve of her ass.

He cursed inwardly and decided they needed to get out of his room asap.

"Did you need to change?" he asked, grabbing his wallet from the desk.

Corinne twirled around to him, causing her dress to flare on her spin. The rotation was like that of a ballet dancer and It only made Xavier's manhood grow more rigid.

"You don't like it?" she asked, almost embarrassed by his question. "I, um, I can change, give me a second." Corinne turned quickly and rushed to the door, but Xavier met her there as if he'd glided on air.

"No," he said with a sigh. "There's nothing wrong with your dress. I apologize."

They shared a look as Xavier searched for the right words. "You are beautiful, and it's my own fault that I feel somewhat out of control with you."

Corinne frowned slightly. "You're out of control with me?" she said. "I was the one that just jumped you in the hallway a few minutes ago."

Xavier's laugh was a grizzly chuckle.

"So I think it's safe to say that I'm out of control with you," she added.

"How about," he slipped his arms around her, "we're both a little on edge." Corinne nodded. "I won't lie to you, Corinne, I've never been in this situation before."

"What situation would that be?"

"In like with someone I barely know."

"Why do you think that is because honestly, I was just trying to figure it out myself."

They both chuckled.

"I'm not sure, but I can't stop myself from wanting to investigate it."

Corinne shuddered in his arms. She would hate to fall in love with Xavier, and he didn't return her sentiments. That would be a disaster. The thought made her want to retreat, but her feet never moved.

"What do you think about that?"

Corinne cleared her throat then smiled. "I'd like that, too."

Xavier exhaled a long breath then his forehead sank into hers. They stared at each other, and the tip of her nose touched the bridge of his. There was a lingering peppermint scent coming from his mouth, and it wrapped around her face and warmed her all over.

"Let's have dinner here," she said. "I don't want to go to a restaurant."

Xavier closed his eyes and pondered on her request. Being in his room was probably not the best idea since he didn't know how much of a stance he could continue to take with her sexy ass modeling around in that dress. He needed to put his mind elsewhere and fast.

"We'll eat on the terrace," he said. Pulling to a stand, Xavier slipped his hand in hers and drew her along the stretch of the room to the double doors. "Give me just a second," he said, leaving her to look out of the windows.

Xavier marched across the suite and found the room service menu. As he ordered a light entrée, his gaze drove from her four-inch heels up her chocolate legs. They disappeared underneath the dress right before he was allowed a look at her plush ass. His body blazed, casting a surrendering heat over his skin; he thought to come out of the shirt, but that consideration was quickly abandoned. It would only intensify things between them, and he was trying to keep it civil.

After ordering, he approached her from behind and paused near her rear. Corinne could feel the heat radiating from his body, and it made her want to fall into the comfort of his chest. Xavier reached around her and slid open the door to the terrace.

"Our dinner will be here shortly."

"Thank you," she said, taking a step out on to the balcony.

Xavier matched her paces, and together they stood side by side overlooking the city.

"Tell me about your childhood, Corinne. I've heard that you were a tomboy, but I can't imagine you that way."

Corinne turned to him with her mouth agape.

"Who told you that?"

Xavier chuckled and slipped a finger down her face then pinched her chin. She shivered but stayed on course with her questioning.

"I have my ways of getting the information I need."

Corinne's mouth was still open.

"The same way you got the information about what flight I would be on?"

"Well, I had to pull out the big guns for that expedition," he said.

Corinne laughed and cut her eyes at him to peer. "Well when I was young, yes, I was a tomboy. I liked playing football, getting dirty and climbing trees." That last statement made Corinne think about climbing Xavier's tree and just that quickly her mind had shifted to the gutter. Her face flushed with a blush, and she bit down on her lip.

"I'm trying to imagine you playing football," he said.

She put her hand on her hip. "You don't think I can?"

Xavier's gaze drove down to meet the connecting limb to her hip, and when he spoke again his voice had grown deeper.

"What would you wear to play football?" As soon as he finished the question, he wondered why he'd asked.

Corinne smirked. "Either a pair of boy shorts or some elastic tights."

Xavier's gaze grew darker. Instead of imagining Corinne as an adolescent with the garment on, he imagined her the way she was now, with all of her thickness stuffed into a pair of elastic tights. To keep his hands to himself, he slipped them inside his pockets and took in a deep breath of fresh air.

"Trust me," Corinne continued, "I was a force to be reckoned with." She smirked over at him.

"I don't doubt it."

"Besides that, I was what they called back in high school a crossover." She went on. "I was book smart and popular. Not that popular people couldn't be smart or vice versa, but in high school, either you were known for your popularity, or you were known for your academics, but never both. But there I was, the prom queen that dated both jocks and nerds, donated to causes I thought were important, and could put the valedictorian out of his misery in a political debate."

"Impressive," he said. "What charities did you donate, too, if you don't mind me asking?"

"When I was fifteen, I started noticing those commercials with the kids that were in other countries. It would say, $38 dollars a month would take care of one kid's nutrition, health insurance, and shelter. I thought about how normal it was for me to have a roof over my head, meals every day and clothes on my back. That was the moment I realized I had to do something. I started a summer job that year working at the zoo. I was only making a few bucks an hour, but I saved my checks and when I had enough, I started sending in $38 dollars a month. I received packets and information on a child I was funding, and it brought tears to my eyes. I was so happy to the point where I imagined one day I would get to meet her.

"What was her name?"

"Natasha Kaweme," she said.

"That's beautiful, and so are you."

Corinne smiled and dropped her eyes. "It felt good, and I was genuinely happy."

He heard the edge that her voice created before she ended the sentence. Seeing the change in her energy, Xavier called out to her. "Corinne, look at me."

Her gaze rose to his. "What happened?" He asked.

Corinne shook her head. "It's childish, as soon as I think, ah, I'm over it, I think about it again and realize there's still some pain there."

Xavier waited for her to go on, keeping her cloaked underneath the drape of his lids.

Corinne shook her head. "It's childish."

"I'm not here to judge you. I just want to know you. That includes everything about you. Hurts, pains, fears," he pulled her close, "challenges, achievements, embarrassing moments." He pulled her closer and smiled and so did she, then they held a long eye on one another. "What happened?"

Corinne sighed. "My uncle Bennie stopped over one day. You know they say everyone has that family member that offers unsolicited advice?"

"Yeah."

"That was Uncle Bennie. He came in and saw me looking over letters and pictures the organization had sent and went into a rant about how I was wasting my money. Those kids weren't being taken care of with the funds I was sending, I was just feeding into a money hungry scheme."

Corinne braced her hands on his chest and pushed off him, slightly removing herself from his arms. She turned and began a slow stroll across the terrace.

"I immediately felt awful. I wanted to call him a liar, but he was so convincing that it broke my spirit. My mother walked in on his ranting, and she kicked him out but never dispelled his points. I was crushed." She paused then turned back around to face him. "Like I said before, childish, right?"

Xavier's face had lost its emotion, and Corinne wondered if she sounded foolish.

"It was childish of your uncle to do that to you, but you can't help who you're kin to."

Corinne nodded. "That is so true."

"Where was she from?"

"Um... Zambia, I recall."

"East Africa?"

"Yes."

"Have you ever been there?"

Corinne's eyes widened, and she blinked like a swiveling Rolodex.

"You're asking me if I've ever been to East Africa?"

"I take that as a no."

An award-winning smile spread across her face. "No, I haven't."

"You seem surprised that I asked. You do have the ability to travel pretty much anywhere with your occupation."

"Yeah, but I'm usually in the same places on rotation. Do you know how incredibly excited I would be to go to Africa?"

Her expression was bright, and the excitement shown tugged at Xavier's heart. "We should go then."

Corinne gawked, thoroughly taken aback. "To East Africa?!"

Xavier chuckled. "You're beginning to sound like a broken record," he said.

"I just, I'm just..." There was a knock on the room door.

"You're just what?"

"Shocked."

"Why?"

"It's not a question I would've ever considered one would ask."

"But you've never been with one like me, either." He moved closer to her. "So, what do you say. Let's go to Africa."

Chills fled down her skin. Xavier wasn't playing games. There was a swift knock on the door again.

"I'll be back," he said, going to grab their room service.

Corinne watched him disappear into the suite and with a hand, she covered her heart. Her mind tossed, going back and forth about being in Zambia. It would give her so much joy to experience the visit that she almost cried. He wouldn't play with her about that, would he? No, of course not, and Corinne would never turn down a trip like that, especially with Xavier.

Chapter Six

When Xavier returned to the terrace with their food, in his hands were two tall candles and two bottles of wine. After turning their tabletop into an elaborate dining experience, Xavier and Corinne sat, prayed, and ate between stealing enticing looks at one another. Corinne couldn't get his proposed trip off her mind, and as she pondered on the possibility, Corinne couldn't take her eyes off the succulent flex of his mouth as he ate. It tickled and warmed her inside, stirring up a rush of chills, unbridled and thick that poured down her skin and wrapped around her groin. She tightened the squeeze on her thighs to keep the pulsation of her pussy from thumping like a wayward woman, but it was no use; Xavier's presence wrecked her nerves, and it was with sheer strength that she didn't jump his bones. Toward the end of their meal, Xavier revisited their conversation before the knock on the door came.

"Would you like some wine?"

Corinne lifted the clothed napkin to the corner of her lips and dabbed.

"I would," she said. She was wondering if he might ask since the bottles had been sitting on ice next to their table since they began eating.

"Red or white? Wait, don't tell me." He studied her a moment longer. "Red," he concluded.

Corinne's eyes arched. "And you would know this because?"

"I've studied the ancient art of women, and there are two types of wine drinkers."

Corinne chuckled. "The ancient art of women?"

Xavier nodded. "For example, most red wine drinkers enjoy dinner by candlelight while white wine drinkers prefer the occasional evening sunset." Xavier rose to his feet, his massive frame covering the table with a midnight shadow. He lifted the bottle of Cabernet Sauvignon while popping the cork. "Red wine drinkers love romance novels while white wine drinkers prefer film festivals." He approached her side of the table and poured the red wine halfway into her glass. Red wine drinkers want to help save the world while white wine drinkers are about family first."

"I think I'd like to be a red and white wine drinker if that's the case," she said. "But I do prefer red over white. You must have graduated from your ancient art of women's studies," she teased.

"Nah, I was just kidding about that part and hoping

whichever one you preferred I'd paint a picture appealing enough for you to feel unique either way."

Corinne tossed her head and laughed, and Xavier released his own grizzly chuckle.

"Well played," she said, still smiling.

Xavier smirked then winked. "You think?"

"Yeah." She lifted the glass to her mouth and took a sip. "You're a smooth operator."

"Only with you."

"Oh, I can hardly believe that."

"It's true, you'll see."

Corinne didn't know how to feel about that response, but without trying, the giddiness on the inside pushed forth to her face, causing heat to balloon in her cheeks. Xavier regained his seat and prompted her.

"So, Ms. Thomas, have you thought about my invitation?"

Corinne twisted her lips and peered at him. "Oh no," she said. "Ms. Thomas makes me feel old."

Xavier chuckled then nodded. "You're right, I should call you Bella anima."

"What does that mean?" she asked, her voice a bit dreamy.

"Beautiful soul. That's what you are. It fits perfectly."

Corinne blushed again. "I think I like that."

"Yeah?"

She nodded, and her cheeks tightened as her blush strengthened.

"Then it's official," he said. "Bella Anima, will you travel across the globe with me on an excursion to explore the motherland?"

Hell yeah, I will. Corinne cleared her throat and took a sip of her wine. Placing the glass back on the table, she brought her sultry stare to him.

"I'd love to." Xavier's growing smile pulled his sexy lips back in a delicious spread; it made Corinne lick her lips. "When do we leave?"

Xavier nodded. "That's my girl," his thick voice cruised.

On the inside, Corinne was enthusiastically excited, and it took everything in her to keep from jumping like a child. Besides, she was a professional that flew across the world just about every day of the week. Even so, she'd never had the pleasure of visiting Africa, and never in a million years did she think it would've been a quest shared with Xavier Valentine. But here she was, with no details and feeling like her younger years, down for whatever, with him.

"How soon can you take time off?"

Corinne relaxed in her seat and swept her hair off her shoulders. "Two weeks."

"One," he countered.

Corinne's brow lifted. "I didn't say two weeks because that's the time I want, it's because that's the standard time-frame for an approval request from Kinship."

Xavier studied her face. "I'll make a call," he said.

Corinne's eyes bucked. "Just like that?"

"Unless of course, you'd rather wait."

"It's not that. I'm just not used to someone stepping in and taking charge so to speak."

"If I've overstepped my boundaries, I apologize." He

paused. "My excuses are selfish." His gaze traveled over her skin. "I want to be with you, Bella anima, sooner rather than later, and I can't explain to you why that desire is so strong right now, but... I'm confident that it will reveal itself in due time. However, I will step out of your way, and let you handle your business, and in two weeks..." He lifted his glass to the air, and Corinne met him halfway in a light cheer, "Africa."

Corinne most certainly wanted to go in one week. But honestly, she needed to wrap her head around what was happening. They sipped their wine, and Xavier sat his glass down and prompted her with another question.

"Tell me, Bella anima, what has been one of the craziest things you've ever done?"

"You first," she responded. "I want to know about your childhood."

Xavier smirked. "Unfortunately, I grew up under the spotlight of the media."

"Unfortunately?"

"Yeah. I don't mean to sound ungrateful so if I do, excuse me. I say unfortunately because I missed out on experiencing a normal childhood. Because of my parents' media enterprise, going to school came with a flared popularity. We were young and accepted the attention in the beginning, but we quickly figured out just because some said they were friends didn't mean they really were."

"Someone betrayed you." It was more of an acknowledgment than a question.

"Plenty," he said. "Especially in college. Some guys would get in trouble and try to use our name to get out of it.

Rumors began to circulate. Whispers about my brothers and I being involved in whatever coup our *friends* were a part of.

"For that reason, we separated ourselves, deciding it was best to stick together. As I told you previously, we were born septuplets, but my youngest brother Trevor didn't survive."

"Oh no, I'm so sorry, Xavier." She reached across the table and covered his brawny hand with hers. Friction slipped through his fingers, but he kept his focus and continued.

"I'd say for the most part I'm good." He gave her a smile that diminished just as quickly as it took shape. "Only when our birthdays roll around do I imagine what he would've looked like and how close we would've been. I'd like to blame Hunter for taking up too much space inside the womb, but it's not a joke I can find myself telling with a whimsical satisfaction."

Corinne smirked and nodded with understanding. "It would've been your way of dealing with it. I'm sure those around you would understand."

He held an eye on her then produced a small smile. "You're probably right."

"Of course, I am," she teased. His smile stretched, and a flurry of butterflies scattered through her stomach.

"I bet you guys had all of the girls after you," she said, easily shifting the subject.

"Why do you think that?"

"Because you're gorgeous."

His gaze dimmed, and it trailed over her lips.

"You think I'm gorgeous, Bella anima?"

Corinne smirked. "I do."

That pair of words forced an image of Corinne in a wedding gown so painstakingly beautiful it stole the next few words Xavier was going to say.

Corinne saw his struggle and responded, "You can't be that surprised."

Xavier blinked. "Um, no… I mean," he exhaled. "Not usually." He revisited his train of thought, trying with urgent haste to shake the images of her at the altar. "My brothers and I were in a b-boy band, so the girls kind of came with the territory."

Corinne's face was bright. "You were in a b-boy band for real?"

Xavier chuckled. "Yeah. We all play different instruments. I was on the drum set while Hunter occasionally played the sax. Lance was the lead guitarist, and DeAndre's superpower was with the microphone."

"He can sing?"

"Better than Maxwell."

"Very interesting. A band of brothers."

Surprise registered across Xavier's face.

"What?" Corinne asked.

"That was our band name."

"You're kidding."

Xavier laughed a hearty guffaw.

"A Band of Brothers."

Corinne's mouth hung open, her eyes wide with heat filling her cheeks. Xavier's million-dollar smile was back, and he reached across the table to drive his fingers down her flushed face.

"Will I ever get to see this in person?" Her excitement boiled over.

"Maybe." He winked.

"Oh come on now, I'm sure my girl Camilla would love to get some sort of doo-wop from you and Hunter."

Xavier's thunderous laugh beat down Corinne's flesh, making her smile harder with wistful joy.

"I'm being so serious right now."

"I know," he said with a grin hanging from his chin. "I'll speak to my brother and see what he says."

"What do you think he'll say?"

"Why the hell did you tell her we were in a b-boy band?" He said, imitating Hunter's voice.

Corinne couldn't help but laugh. She fell against her chair and serenaded him with her heavy chortle. "No, he wouldn't!" she countered. "Hunter's a sweetheart."

Xavier's brows knocked together in a frown. "Hunter is a vile human being. Anyone would be lucky to steer clear of him."

Corinne shook her head, retaining the smile on her face.

"No, I'm just messing around. He'll be down."

Corinne shook her head and pointed at Xavier. "You've got a lot of jokes tonight."

"I just love seeing you smile."

She blushed. "And I love seeing yours."

He wiggled his brow. "You've told me I was gorgeous, now you're telling me you love my smile. Jesus, woman, if you keep stroking my ego, I'll be forced to wrap you up in my arms and kiss you to death."

His voice stroked her flesh, and Corinne's cheeks filled

with more intense heat. A nervous laugh trickled from her. "You're silly."

"Silly serious," he said.

Corinne lifted her glass and took down the rest of her wine, the liquid courage giving her the strength to move forward.

"Maybe I'll let you."

Xavier pulled his bottom lip between his teeth. "A kiss can land us in a dangerous place," he said. "I'm not sure you want to be there."

Corinne slid her chair back and rose to her feet. She moved away from the table and sauntered the few steps to approach him.

"Try me."

Chapter Seven

Xavier's blood heated and the hairs on his forearms lifted. A vanilla bean fragrance wafted from her, disturbing the natural order of his senses. With his nerves in a frenzy now, he took a gaze from her high heel shoes, up her bare legs, across the valley that remained hidden from him behind her summer dress to her breasts. They puckered high and mighty behind the thin material, boastful in their stance and coated with a brown-layered glaze that was her skin. At her lips, Xavier stopped breathing. Her body was a sight to behold, but her face was so elegantly fashioned that he was certain the creator spun her with molded precision.

A delightful array of passionate energy seized him, rendering Xavier speechless. "Bella Anima… you shouldn't test this concept. There's only so many times I can stop myself."

Corinne realized this kiss would go beyond a mere

smooch on the lips, but damn if she didn't want it. Because she did. Corinne licked her mouth and took a few steps backward until her derriere bumped against the railing. Xavier seized that opportunity to stand, and on his feet, he strolled up to her, bringing an intense heat that paralyzed her thoughts. Leaning forward, he locked each hand on both sides of the railing, sealing Corrine in.

"Never mind what I said before," he said. Xavier dipped to her mouth and captured her lips in a kiss so profound that it rocked them both. Corinne's legs weakened, and she nearly collapsed, but Xavier caught her fall with an arm that glided around her waist and pulled her flank against the ridges of his chest. The kiss was heavenly, like some sort of enchanted supremacy that cast an incantation she had no power of pulling from. He tasted her full mouth, trailing his tongue over her lips and dancing in a fox-trot with her tongue. Heat ballooned in them both, and just when Xavier began to melt into her skin, he withdrew; breaths bated and chests rising and falling.

"I don't know if we should do that too many more times. It's becoming my addiction," he announced.

Corinne couldn't agree or disagree. She could only hold steady while she fought interactively to breathe in and out. She was dizzy, and though Xavier was right, she didn't want him to be.

"Are you all right?"

Corinne nodded, still refusing to use her voice. Xavier regarded her.

"Certain?"

Corinne nodded again. "I've got to be honest here,

Xavier," she started, "I don't know how we can keep our hands off of each other. There seems to be something that overpowers me when we're together."

"So I'm not the only one then."

She shook her head. "No."

"How long have you felt this way?"

Corinne swallowed, and they both responded at the same time.

"From the day we met."

Their gazes held firm, and their breathing tingled each other's mouths. They were too close, and both fighting temptation. Corinne was trying to talk herself out of jumping him again. He'd already been the one to stop their lovemaking the first time, but if she did it again, he might not. That wasn't the problem. Would she regret it? Corinne wanted to see this thing through. She was desperate to know if their close friendship would turn into a real relationship. It wasn't impossible, but if they had sex he might not be as attracted to her as he was now.

Her thoughts went back and forth as she stared, watching his gaze tour over the elements of her face. Xavier was going through much of the same battle, except he felt the need to hold off until he heard her say those words. I trust you. It would be the only thing that would break his fortitude. He kissed her lips softly then pulled upright and took a step back.

Corinne blinked then glanced around as if coming out of her own dream.

"It's getting late," she said, looking for a reason to leave his presence, so she could hide.

"You're right," he agreed.

"I should probably get going, and we'll reconvene in the morning."

"I'll walk you to your door."

Corinne nodded and pushed off the railing. Xavier slipped to her side, allowing her to walk past him back into his suite. As she meandered through, she couldn't help but notice the door against the wall. She paused then turned to him.

"Adjoining rooms?"

"Yes, you're okay with that, aren't you?"

"Yeah, I just heard you talking earlier after I'd gotten out of the shower, so I thought I would ask."

Xavier's mind assaulted him with images of Corinne nude and wet. His dick bounced in his pants, and he almost cursed up a storm at his unfiltered thoughts.

"Hmmm," was all he said.

Corinne continued to the door with Xavier pacing her steps. He reached around and opened it, and they took the short walk to her room.

"If you need anything, you don't have to bear the journey of coming to this door or knocking on the other, just come," he said.

Corinne's chest swelled. She knew what he meant. Xavier was talking in reference to the adjoining door, and she nodded and smiled.

"Thank you for dinner, and taking time out of your busy schedule to hang out with me. I know that isn't easy with how in demand you are."

"You don't have to thank me, Bella anima, there's no

place else I'd rather be." He pulled his sexy lip in with his teeth, and Corinne turned from him quickly and fumbled out her key. She entered the door fast in her last attempt to not escape Xavier but escape her own wrestling. Being around him was uncanny, and until she could get a hold of herself, she should probably stay away. *Yeah, like that's going to happen.*

Corinne leaned a shoulder against the door and dropped her head. Her nerves had been shaken up so many times in one day she felt she would burst at any moment. She lifted her head and peered out the peephole to see if he was still there, but the only thing she saw was the door across the hall.

"Thank God," she whispered. Had Xavier actually been there, Corinne would've said fuck it.

"This is so ridiculous," she said.

The last time Corinne felt this horny around a man was, was... she tossed her hands up; she couldn't put a mark on that either.

Feeling completely unraveled and frustrated, Corinne stalked from the door, and with every step she took, she removed an item. Her shoes were the first to go, then her dress, bra, and panties. Before she could stop herself, she was on her back splayed out across the bed with her fingers pressed against her clitoris.

"Aaaaaah," she crooned at the stimulating sweep against her sensitive flesh. Her fingers flipped and flickered her clit, and her feet dug into the bed as her hips rotated.

"Ssssss... aaah, oh God," she panted.

Her heartbeat raced, and in the depths of her passionate

self-love, she saw his face, brown skin smooth without flaw, thick lips, soft and inviting, that long ass beard and a mustache that was groomed around the outline of his mouth. She imagined her tongue tasting his as he stared her down behind the dark molasses of his brown eyes.

"Shit!" she panted. Her pussy thumped rigorously, and she was about to come in a landslide. "Xavier, Xavier...," she purred, imagining him slipping down her belly, his tongue gliding over her peach just before sucking it completely then stirring her with one long intense stroke of his tongue.

"Aaaah!"

She came, so hard her thighs clapped together and sealed her hand inside the apex of her legs.

"Jesus!"

Her eyes crossed, and her ears popped as a wave of nostalgia cast her afloat just as her body went limp. Her breathing was haggard, but Corinne couldn't move as if Xavier had really put it on her. Her ears popped and not a minute after her release she passed out and slept through the night.

Chapter Eight

The breeze in the early morning atmosphere gave off an unordinary chill as the drop-top Ferrari sailed down the street. Corinne shivered while telling herself the change in her ecosystem had everything to do with the weather and not the man sitting next to her.

This morning when she'd awakened and found herself butt naked with her feminine scent on her fingers, Corinne could do nothing but laugh and roll her face into the pillows. Her phone buzzed, indicating a notification on her screen. She reached for the device and pulled it underneath the pillow to read a text message from Xavier.

"Good morning, Bella Anima. I'd like to begin our morning in an hour if that's all right with you."

Corinne's eyes traveled to the time. 4:30 a.m. Where the hell were they going this early, she wondered.

"Good morning, in one hour I'm all yours."
Send.
"I like the sound of that."

Corinne blushed and stuffed her face back into the pillow. The sun wasn't even out, but here he was ready to be in her company again. She mused on those thoughts and laid for another thirty minutes before getting up and making her way into the shower. Her midnight solo tryst was necessary to take the edge off, as was the one she'd taken in the shower. Corinne was hoping by getting that out of the way, she could focus on whatever adventure Xavier had set for them that morning before it was time to head back to the airport. However, when the three-knuckle knock came on the door, Corinne became instantly nervous and thrilled altogether. She checked her appearance one last time before opening the door. Her look was simple but chic.

Her vintage style peach sunglasses added an extra flair of bravura to the peach jumpsuit she wore. A rugged black belt accented her waist while large black buttons ran down the middle of her one-piece. On her feet black thong sandals complemented her pedicured toes, and her brown shea butter skin gave the entire look a pop of praise. Satisfied, she'd sauntered to open the door and was hit with a conglomerate of instant heat at the modest yet evocative look of Xavier Valentine.

He too wore aviator shades across his eyes, but it didn't stop Corinne from feeling the laser-like beam his orbs traced over her entire body. Her gaze soaked him up, all six feet three inches of his vigorous frame. His hands were connected behind his back, making his broad shoulders push through the Fendi shirt he wore even more than usual. The material was no match for his sturdy build as his chiseled chest made a statement that was defined by the ripples in his solidly built torso. The jeans that crossed his herculean thighs put all denim to shame as they rode his limbs like they were tailored to fit his colossal frame. They thinned off at his ankles where a pair of Nikes congregated at his feet. Xavier removed his sunglasses and tucked the lens to grip the middle of his shirt while burning a hole into her eyes with his compelling gaze. Corinne tried to pay attention to her breathing pattern, but this man was finer than fine. Sinfully so. It was the thick chocolatiness of his skin and the way his Adam's apple bobbled that discombobulated her.

"Good morning," his dark voice drummed. "Are you ready?"

He licked his lips, and Corinne's hands searched for pearls to clutch when she realized she wasn't wearing any. *Holy Spirit, hold me.*

"Yes," she said.

"I'll take your bag."

Corinne barely heard his response, but she handed over the bag in question as if her subconscious was making decisions on her behalf. Xavier held the door open as she exited, and they strolled down the hallway to the elevators.

"Did you sleep well?" he asked.

The doors dinged, and they stepped on.

"Like a baby," she said having her own little inside joke. *If only he knew.*

Now, they were on the road to someplace Corinne didn't know about. She felt free, and it was different from the freedom her anonymous persona took on during her layovers.

"What are you thinking?" Xavier asked, snapping her out of her reverie.

She stretched her arms over her head then straightened and glanced at him. "How calm and easygoing my spirit feels right now. It's wonderful, and I wish I felt this way all the time."

"How do you usually feel?"

"Rushed," she admitted, "like I'm always on go. I guess in hindsight I am, and although it can be fun at times, it can also be lonely and tiresome. I look forward to the day I can relax at home with my family or even have a family to come home to. I don't mean my parents' either."

Xavier smiled back at her. "Maybe we can do something about that."

A comprehensive heat warmed her skin.

"Oh yeah?" She smiled, looking over at him.

Xavier nodded. "Hell yeah," his deep voice bellowed. Her eyes traced his wide smile, pearly teeth and that delicious mouth.

Corinne's nipples tightened, and she inwardly reprimanded herself. *Oh, hell no, don't you get all horny again, haven't you had enough?*

"Why do you think you feel that way now?"

He turned down a boulevard that was light on traffic.

"Hmmm?" Corinne said.

"You said your spirit feels calm and easygoing, why do you think that is?"

"Oh, I'm not sure yet, but I notice it's not the same as… as…"

Xavier glanced at her. "As what?"

Corinne sighed. "Remember last night when you asked me what the craziest thing was I'd ever done?"

"Yes."

"Okay, well, I'm not that wild of a person."

Xavier laughed. "Starting with that line makes me think otherwise."

"No," she chuckled, "seriously, I usually play by the rules, but since I've been a stewardess, on my layovers, and I mean the extended ones not the ones that only last a few hours, I change into someone else. It's freeing but feels nothing like I feel now."

"When you say change into someone else, you mean…"

"Oh," she laughed. "It's nothing big, I just pretend I'm someone else. I usually use the name Angela Spears when I'm asked by locals around me, or especially if a guy is trying to hold a conversation. There's this one guy, Carlos, every time I'm staying over in Anguilla, he surfaces. I think he likes me, but there are a few like him in other places I frequent. I give him small conversation then go on about my business. Sometimes, I ignore them. Not on purpose, but my name's not really Angela, so I find myself going, huh, oh, hi!" She laughed and shook her head.

Xavier took in that information with unsettling awareness.

"It's not that I'm trying to trick anyone or anything, God, I must sound loco. It's my own way of being safe actually. You never know who people are or what their intentions may be. Giving out your real name and information could be hazardous."

Xavier nodded in understanding as he made another turn into an open field area. He parked and shut the engine off then rotated to her.

"Listen." He cupped her chin and stared into her eyes. "I want you to be careful when you're on these layovers. Maybe you could take one of the other stewardesses with you when you're staying overnight somewhere. It's always safer to travel with another person than on your own. And another thing, I do understand your reasoning for with-holding your personal information, but think about giving someone you can trust, like a security officer at your hotel or even a bartender on the beach your real name. That way it'll be sort of a checkpoint of your whereabouts should, God forbid, something happen to you."

She saw his jaw tighten and completely melted at the troubled expression on his face. She reached for his beard, and her hand slipped up to caress his face.

"You're worried about me," she crooned.

He turned his face into her palm and kissed the thread of her fingers.

"Promise me you will."

A sprinkling web of heat sprouted over her fingers as his mouth kissed each one with tender care.

"I promise," she said.

He grabbed her hand and held on tight.

"Thank you."

She blushed, and he slipped out of the driver's seat, materializing at her passenger door. He opened it swiftly and helped her out, and together they strolled across the meadow of green grass and trailed up a slope. In the short distance, Corinne could see a man standing with equipment around his feet. His hands were on his hips, and he waved over with a huge smile on his face. She glanced over at Xavier.

"Okay, I've got to ask. What's going on here?"

Xavier barked out a laugh. "I'm surprised you're just now asking me that question."

"Well at first, I wasn't worried, but now I don't know."

Xavier laughed harder as they approached the middle-aged man.

"I promise to take good care of you," Xavier said. He offered his hand to the man, and it was accepted with a firm shake. "Good morning," Xavier said.

"Good morning, Mr. Valentine." The man looked at Corinne. "Good morning."

"Corinne Thomas," Xavier introduced.

"Ms. Thomas, I'm Stan Bradford. It's nice to meet you."

Corinne took note of Stan's appearance. She wasn't into stereotypes, but he gave the impression of a middle-aged, athletic, instructor of some sort with his fitted jeans, closed toe boots, and cocky stance. She reached for his butterscotch hand and shook it.

"You, too, Mr. Bradford."

"Oh, call me Stan. I hear Xavier is taking you for a nice ride this early morning."

Corinne glanced at Xavier. "Well, you've heard more than me," she said.

"Oops." Stan covered his mouth.

"It's quite all right. I have her here now. She can't run."

Corinne's eyes widened. It was then that she glanced around at the equipment in front of them.

"Xavier... what is this?"

"We're going paragliding, Bella anima."

Corinne's eyes lurched. "Paragliding? As in hang gliding?"

"Something like that but not quite," Stan cut in. "You see with hang gliding, you're laying down stretched out with a sail and a crossbar. You would also need to be at a higher altitude. With paragliding you're sitting upright inside of this."

Stan reached for a piece of equipment that looked like a seat made with the curve of a banana. "This is your harness. Mr. Valentine knows what he's doing, but let me give you a quick lesson on how this works." Stan glanced at Xavier. "Unless you'd like to show her."

"By all means," he said, prompting Stan to continue.

"Paragliding is a non-mechanical foot-launch method of free-flying with this here expandable lightweight wing. I'll simply hook up your gear, and after the wing is inflated, your pilot here will take a small spirited jog down this slope. The wing will catch a current, and you'll be lifted into the air. He then sits inside this harness while you'll be sitting in one just like it practically in his lap."

Corinne shivered, and she couldn't blame it on the chill since the breeze felt more like warm wind. "Okay..." she said.

"Usually you would jog with him, but I think Mr. Valentine wants to pilot this thing alone."

"I'll get her help on the landing. I think it's something she would love to do." Xavier looked at Corinne. "If you'd rather try another venture entirely, I have an alternative idea in mind," Xavier said, "but I would love it if you would ride the waves of the skyline with me."

He reached out and grabbed her hand, intertwining their fingers. Corinne smirked. "Let's do it," she said feeling brave. "I'm a stewardess, I fly high for a living, babe."

Xavier's hearty laugh sent a tinkle of chills down her skin, and she squeezed his hand. He in turn pulled her close, wrapping her in the safety net of his chest where he placed warm tender kisses down her nose then her lips.

"Mmmm, don't start, Mr. Valentine, it's too early," she said.

"It's never too early for a little love on the side of a slope."

Corinne laughed, and Xavier smiled lustrously.

Stan cleared his throat. "I don't mean to interrupt this fond moment, but Mr. Valentine if you'd like to get that view we spoke about yesterday, now would be the time to prepare."

Xavier quickly unraveled them. "Sure thing."

He pulled Corinne over to the equipment, and with Stan's help, they began getting assembled.

"What view?" Corinne said. "It's still dark. I can barely see anything a few feet ahead. "Speaking of which, shouldn't there be some sort of flashlights or something?"

Xavier and Stan chuckled. "I'll let Mr. Valentine give you the specifics," Stan said.

Corinne glanced back at Xavier. "Well?"

Xavier took his hands over her connectors, making sure they were tightly in place. "Get in, and I'll show you."

Corinne climbed into the harness and was pleasantly surprised at how comfortable the seat was. Xavier continued connecting her inside, pulling on her straps to make sure they were tight.

"I'm definitely not falling out of this thing," she said.

He chuckled. "Not at all." Xavier glanced over at Stan. "Stan, my man, thank you, brother." He reached out, and he and Stan slapped hands.

"Anytime. Do your thing."

Xavier turned back to Corinne. "You ready, Bella anima?"

"As ready as I'll ever be."

Without a second thought, Xavier took a few steps and the shift caused the wing to fly high like a hot air balloon. Three dashing steps later his feet left the ground, and they were airborne as the pockets of heat cast them to the clouds. Corinne squealed.

"Oh my God!"

An exuberant force of energy spiraled through her core, making her nerves stand on edge. They floated higher.

"This is amazing!"

Xavier smiled and leaned closer to her ear then spoke, sending another vibrant tingle coursing through her from the heat of his mouth.

"Have you ever seen a sunset at night, Bella anima?"

"Um... yes," she said.

"How about a sunrise?"

Just as the words left his lips, the sun broke the firmament, peaking its rays across the heavens inch by inch. It took on a vivacious illumination, offering the couple a rare look at the entire valley as if the valley itself were waking up from slumber. Surrounding them were mountains and hills, some tall and others slim. The shape of them as if they'd been carved by the skilled hands of an architect making the diagrams of a structure. Below green grass stretched for miles on end all while they navigated the thermals of the sun-soaked terrestrial underneath.

"Xavier, this is beautiful," Corinne crooned, her eyes wide and taking in every inch of the panoramic view in front of her. She would've loved to take out her cell phone and snap a picture, but she was afraid to draw her eyes off the scenery for even a second.

"Would you like to pilot us?"

"Huh, oh, no way!"

Xavier laughed. "Why not, Bella? I believe you can do it."

"Ha! Maybe you shouldn't!"

Xavier laughed again. "Come on, it's not so bad. Here, we'll do it together." Xavier placed her hand underneath his and easily sailed the aerodynamically shaped wing.

"Oh my gosh!"

Xavier chuckled. "See that's not so bad, is it?"

The balloon twirled them, making Corinne laugh from the tickling sensation of butterflies in her stomach.

"This is so serene!"

Xavier's face warmed as he watched her light up like Christmas morning. A tug in his chest made his heart race, and for a second, he almost forgot he was the pilot. Pulling his eyes back to the landscape, he guided them over the valley for a long stretch until they came upon their landing. Corinne was so captured by the full effect of the trip that she pouted when it was time for it to end.

"Already?" she whined.

Xavier chuckled. "You've got a flight to catch, love. We should get going unless of course you want to stay a little longer."

"No, no, you're right, I guess."

"Don't be so down, Bella anima. We're two weeks away from Africa, surely we can find a spot there to glide."

Corinne cocked her head to the side to look at him. "Don't play with me!"

Xavier chuckled, amused by her animation.

"I wouldn't dare."

Corinne's cheeks hurt they were tightly inflated with a blush.

"In thirty seconds," Xavier began, "we're going to both pull our feet forward and jump out running. It will be just like our beginning, but it'll be up to us to slow the pace. You ready?"

She tossed her head back and smiled. "Yes!"

"Okay, here we go."

Xavier and Corinne looked on with exuberant concentration as the wind sailed the hot air balloon toward the ground.

He began counting down. "Five, four, three, two, one!"

Corinne squealed, and they both jumped, their feet touching the ground in a fast sprint. The laughter bubbling from Corinne was out of control. She was completely tickled by their landing. As their feet shuffled to a stop, Xavier ran into her, cloaking Corinne with a wrapping of his arms.

"Come here you," he said, sealing them instantly together. His mouth found her face, and throat, and her arms slipped around his neck. She laughed while moaning simultaneously from the friction his mouth caused against her skin.

"Xavier…"

A guttural growl drummed from him. "Don't say my name like that."

"Or what, hmm?"

"Or you'll miss your flight."

A thrill of chills circled her skin, and her nipples became tight until the point where they ached. *Lord, have mercy.*

"It's your fault this time," she practically huffed. "You were the one that started this."

"You're right, and I'll finish it, too."

He kissed alongside her jaw.

"Xavier…"

He lifted her completely, heavy equipment be damned.

"Okay, okay!" she squealed. He replaced her on her feet and reluctantly let her go. "That was so fun. How do we get this stuff off?"

Xavier laughed and went about the task of unclamping her equipment.

"Are you going back to Chicago, or do you have somewhere else to be?"

"I'll be in Chicago for a week, then Australia for another, then Africa."

He winked, and she returned the gesture with a smirk.

"Okay, then maybe I'll get to see you next week."

"Bella, we won't be one of those couples who have to schedule each other in for personal time."

His words took her by surprise.

"Are we a couple, Xavier?"

He stopped unclasping the equipment long enough to hold a steady gaze on her.

"Would you like that, Corinne?"

She blushed. "Would you?"

Xavier chuckled. "Yes." He reached for her hand and entwined their fingers again. "I'd like to court you, officially."

"Oh, court me, you're gonna go old school on me, huh?"

He chuckled again and tweaked her cheek with his fingers.

"All right," she said, "maybe I'd like to court you," Her smile was just as dazzling as the last one she offered him.

"That means no flirting with other men on these extended layovers of yours."

Corinne gasped, and a smile stretched wide across her face.

"They flirt with me!"

Xavier nodded. "And you don't flirt back?"

"Well, I, um."

"Mmhmm, don't lie to me, girl."

Corinne laughed. "Okay, you got me. No flirting, not that I would when I'm dating someone."

"That's good to know."

A Jeep Wrangler pulled up on them with Stan behind the wheel.

"You folks need a lift back to your car?" he asked. "Don't worry about the equipment. Jenna my assistant will be here shortly to gather everything."

"Right on time," Xavier said.

They removed the rest of the equipment then climbed into the backseat together where Corinne sat in the cocoon of Xavier's chest. His arm was thrown across her shoulders, and they both felt a building desire for the future of their relationship. It was almost too good to be true, but however long this bliss would last, they were excited to be in it together.

Chapter Nine

heir farewell was bittersweet, but Corinne was holding on to every inch of their time together. She stood next to the microphone onboard Kinship Airlines ready to make her official welcome speech. It had only been thirty minutes since she and Xavier parted. He was very old school, wanting to make sure she was on board safely before sprinting across the airport to catch his flight.

"You're going to be late," she argued. "You'll miss your flight!"

"There will be another," he responded.

Corinne couldn't say much after that. Xavier wasn't budging, and his attention made her long for him all the more.

"Are you going to use that thing?"

Corinne blinked and turned to Monica, the stewardess who had caught she and Xavier's kiss the day before.

"Oh yeah, but if you want it, go right ahead." Corinne slid to the side, and Monica took her spot. Monica lifted the intercom and spoke through the mic. As she welcomed the guests aboard flight 132, Corinne drifted off again. She thought of Xavier's smile and the way he touched her while they were together. It was either with a fierce gripping or a tender brush. It made her body dredge up a strenuous fever, and the heat was impossible to contain.

"Corinne."

Corinne snapped from her thoughts again. "Hmm?"

"Where are you. It's time to take our seats before this flight takes off."

"Oh." Corinne shook her head. "I'm sorry, was just a little lost in thought."

"It's Xavier, isn't it?"

Corinne and Monica weren't the best of friends. Their relationship didn't go further than the necessary tolerance one would have for a coworker. Corinne was reminded of Xavier's request then. He wanted her to travel with a stewardess on her layovers. Maybe she should get better acquainted with Monica.

"I'm not sure if you're aware," Monica began, "but Xavier is a frequent flyer of the mile-high club. You would do good not to take him seriously. Women should only want to be with a man like him for pleasure. Anything past that is putting your heart on the line, and who has time for that, right?"

Just that quick, Corinne was backtracking on her getting to know Monica thoughts.

"And how would you know he's a frequent flyer of the mile-high club?"

Monica shrugged. "Girl, everybody knows. Xavier doesn't usually fly commercial. He has his own private jet, and he's been spotted plenty of times getting on and off with some model on his arm. I've even seen pictures of him with that princess, what's her name?" Monica snapped her fingers. "Nadine Benson! The daughter of—"

"I know whose daughter she is," Corinne snapped.

Monica shut her lips tight. "I didn't mean to rub you the wrong way—"

"Oh really?" Corinne said, being sarcastic. "So, you thought telling me that the man I'm dating is a womanizer and enjoys sexing said women on his private jet wouldn't rub me the wrong way?"

Monica shut her lips even tighter.

"What? I can't hear you," Corinne went on.

"I— I was just trying to look out for you."

"Why, because we're friends? Because the last time I checked, you haven't spent a lunch break worth of period conversing with me much less getting to know me well enough to say you're just looking out for me. You're trying to be a bitch, and you can save it for someone who cares about your opinion."

Corinne walked away with her head held high and her attitude just as elevated. She found the stewardess chair and buckled up then turned her attention to the empty seat that sat a few feet in front of her. The one Xavier previously occupied. A headache had taken root, and now her morning had just been stepped all over by Monica and her unwarranted advice. Corinne needed to talk to a real friend. She would be off at the end of the week for a few days, and she planned to take advantage. A little R and R with Camilla should do the trick. If she could pull Camilla away from Hunter for a second.

"ARE WE STILL ON FOR THE MEETING?"

Xavier flipped his wrist and checked the time on his Rolex as he spoke into the phone.

"Yeah, I'm heading there now," Hunter said.

Slipping into the driver seat of his Jaguar, Xavier attached his cell to the pro clip dashboard mount and the Bluetooth connected automatically.

"How do you expect this conversation will go?" He asked.

Hunter sighed on the other end. "We have something they want, and they have something we want, so I'm hoping we could come to an agreement."

Xavier nodded and shifted gears as he headed downtown for the private assembly.

"We haven't had much luck in the past getting them to bite."

"We hadn't had anything they wanted either. We'll see how it goes. How close are you now?"

"Not that far, six minutes give or take."

"All right, I'll see you there."

Their line disconnected, and Xavier pondered on the gathering that would surely turn the heads of the media. He could almost see the headlines now. Switching lanes, he pushed a heavy foot on the pedal and shot down the fast track of the freeway in record time. At the exit, he easily guided the purring engine of the Jag through the downtown streets before coming to a red light. Corinne was never too far away from his thoughts, and it was becoming more recurrent. In fact, everything about his attraction to Corinne was rare specifically because he'd never felt such a strong connection to any woman, except…

There was that one time Xavier thought he'd found someone special. Nadine Benson. She'd been there from the beginning of his career and stuck around during his early bachelor days. At one time he would've considered her the one, but Xavier's eyes had been open after a phone conversation that ended sweet but turned sour.

"Oh yeah, how bad do you miss me," Xavier had asked Nadine.

"So bad I'm currently tracking the GPS in your car right now."

Xavier's smile turned into a frown. "Say what?"

Nadine laughed. "I'm just kidding, I would never do something so childish and insecure."

"That's good to know."

The line beeped. "Oh, sweetheart, let me call you back. This is my mother calling, and she'd be a complete damsel if I don't answer."

Xavier chuckled. "Take your call. I'll talk to you later."

"Smooches," Nadine said.

Xavier sent a loud smack of a kiss through the phone, and Nadine giggled then clicked over to her mom.

"Yes, Mother, how are you tonight?"

"I'm fine dear, how are you and the benefactor?"

Nadine laughed. "Mom, you are ridiculously funny. My benefactor has a name, he goes by Xavier Valentine. And we're fine, why do you ask?"

"I always ask."

"But why do you always ask, Mother? I think it's becoming an obsession of yours."

"I've always thought you were too good for the likes of Xavier Valentine. Your royalty, sweetheart, and those Valentine men are…" Nadine's mom let out a scathing sound. "Not worthy. That's the most pleasant way for me to describe them. For all the time you've stood by his side, and I do mean side in every aspect of the word since he let you watch him fool around with other women."

"Mother, he was single," Nadine cut in.

Nadine's mother scoffed. "Single my ass. Anyone with eyes that could see would know you guys were together. But that's okay, your payday is coming. Once he signs that famous soccer player, I can never remember his name," her mother mumbled, "you'll be rolling in dough."

"True," Nadine added. "But we're royalty, we've always been rolling in dough."

"Mmhmm, but more is always better, and I can't wait for you to become Mrs. Valentine so you can take him to the bank. Make sure to put every asset in your name."

"I've got this covered, Mother, I don't need your instruction."

"Of course you do. You are your mother's daughter, and I've taught you well. If your father even thought about leaving me today, he'd walk away with fifty cents because I would hold the power to everything."

The two women laughed, amused with their antics. There was just one problem; Xavier's phone hadn't hung up. It was still connected and had crossed over into their conversation. They couldn't hear him, but he heard every word they'd spoken through his earpiece. He couldn't deny he was heartbroken. As long as he'd known Nadine, he was sure if anyone was with him for the right reasons it was her. But he was a fool, and according to her mother, he didn't even have a name. The benefactor. That's what he'd been reduced to.

That day changed the dynamic of the way he thought about women. Whenever one would seek him out for pleasure or otherwise, he considered them long enough to be eye candy for the media, then he would drop them off at home on his way to his estate. His heart hadn't been open for business since then, but the blind date with Corinne shifted his atmosphere completely. The comfort he felt with her he'd never felt with anyone, not even Nadine. He was still trying to figure it out, but while he did so, Xavier couldn't stop himself from enjoying her company and he wouldn't.

That unfortunate incident didn't remove Xavier from Nadine's radar. Before this morning's meeting he'd caught a glimpse of her on T.V. As he flipped through the channels, a segment on a daytime talk show caught his eye.

"We were sure there was a romance brewing between you and Xavier Valentine," the host said. "Care to share whatever happened between you two?

Nadine Benson smiled softly as her sharp eyes and fierce shoulder length haircut bounced as she shifted in her seat.

"Xavier was someone special," her voice was low and thoughtful. "The demise of our relationship was my fault and I'll always regret that."

"That's unfortunate," the host said. "Any possibility of rekindling that lost love."

Nadine smiled softly again. "If so, you'll be the first to know..."

Xavier had stood before the television watching her put on the show of a lifetime. It would be a long day in hell before he decided to give her a second chance. The conversation between Nadine and her mother floated back to him. *Disgusting*, he thought, shaking off the unpleasant occurrence.

Xavier drove the Jag into an underground garage and exited swiftly. It was Friday afternoon, three days since his paragliding adventure with Corinne. He smiled thinking about how giddy she became while they flew. Her voice tickled his ears as he hit the elevator button and stepped on headed for the top floor. The private crane sailed expeditiously to the top, and he strolled confidently off when the doors dinged then open. The few people in the office turned to stare at him as he made his way through the bank's branch, and he smiled optimistically as he approached the office at the end of the hall.

Xavier lifted his hand and knocked in rhythm.

"Come in," a voice boomed from inside.

Xavier opened the door and stepped into the conference room then closed the door behind himself. Nine pairs of eyes connected with his, and a formal smile glittered across his handsome face, as he tilted his head in a nod.

"It appears that I'm late," Xavier said. "I apologize, I'm running from one meeting to the next."

"It's no problem, son," Leslie Valentine said. The older man's dark brown eyes zoomed in on Xavier's spiffy white suit. Xavier had always thought his father's all black hair with that one fat strand of gray falling down the side made him look like one of the X-Men. It had been a joke of Xavier's and their brothers for as long as he could remember. However, his father would respond with a snide comment that would make them all want to regurgitate their lunch like "Your mothers never complained once, as a matter of fact, she pulls on this gray—" and they would always scream to stop him.

That always gave Leslie a sense of pleasure to see his sons squirm. "Looks like the jokes on you," he would say.

Xavier combed an eye over Leslie; he was dapper in a formal tux that Xavier had never seen before. Must have been new. His father's physique carried just as much strength as his sons and his fingers were linked sitting comfortably on the table top.

"Your brothers and I were just catching up with Christopher Lee Rose and his sons."

Xavier glanced around the room to the Rose men. Of the ones in attendance, Xavier was well aware of their accolades.

Jonas Alexander Rose was a former undefeated heavyweight champion and Chairman & CEO at Rose Bank and Trust Credit Union.

Jaden Alexander Rose was Jonas' business partner and most sought-after investment banker. Jaden had been named on Forbes 30 under 30 finance list as one of the youngest traders, bankers, and dealmakers. He currently ran his own $730 million-dollar hedge fund at Rose Bank and Trust Credit Union.

Jonathon Alexander Rose was the head honcho at Rose Security Group, a private company that offered a range of manpower services to government and high-profile clients. It was currently the number one security firm operating across the east coast region.

Jordan Alexander Rose was partner at Rose and Garnet LLC, the highest paid attorneys at law with the most prestigious client list.

Christopher Lee Rose, their father, mentor, the previous owner of Rose Bank and Trust Credit Union, and Gemz, the multimillion dollar chewing gum company sat at the head of the table while Leslie Valentine was parked at the other end.

Next to Leslie was Xavier's brothers. Hunter Valentine, CEO of VFC Energy, a fortune 500 company. VFC had been named alongside Rose Bank and Trust Credit Union as one of the most respected companies in Chicago.

Lance Valentine was an award-winning film director and one of the best working in Hollywood with a number of commercially successful and critically acclaimed credits.

Kyle Valentine was the youngest top software engineer of his time. He had cofounded Zing the popular search engine in 1996.

Lastly, Leslie Valentine, Xavier's father, powerhouse and media mogul of four influential television news stations.

There were over a billion dollars in the room and a significant reason security was set up outside of the bank so tightly. While almost everyone was seated, Xavier noticed Hunter wasn't, choosing to stand next to their father. His posture was perfect, upright with an aerial view of everyone in the room, almost as if he felt threatened. But he wasn't the only one on his feet. Across the table, Jonas also stood much the same way except his hands were tucked easily inside his pockets. The men were all dressed in suits. Some Armani, Brioni, Tom Ford, and the like. Cufflinks, ties, and gleaming belt buckles accessorized their attire. While loafers, oxfords, and wingtip shoes dressed their feet.

Xavier strolled to the empty chair in the room and paused, then took an eye over to Hunter. Hunter nodded as if to say, everything is good, and Xavier took his seat.

"Now that we're all here, let's get right to it," Leslie Valentine said. Leslie gave Christopher eye contact. "I know we've had our differences in the past, but—"

"You call purposefully undermining us to sneak your bids on the Lotus housing development at the last second differences? You knew the sale was a done deal, but like a snake, you slithered over to the associate with your smooth talk, throwing an asinine amount of money on the table to steal it right from underneath our noses."

It was Jaden who'd spoken.

"It's the cost of doing business," Lance intervened. "That's how you win a bid when the competition is sleeping."

It was a direct hit, and the Rose men felt it.

"However," Lance continued. "This development we have decided to come to you with a proposal and not sneak as you put it, and steal it from underneath your noses. But," he went on, "we could if you'd prefer it."

Another direct hit, and Jonas was done playing games just that quick.

"Are you willing to fight for it?" Jonas said.

All eyes on the Valentine's side of the table went to him, each of them wondering if he was speaking in reference to a bidding war or a physical fight.

Hunter responded, "You know Jonas, I know you're undefeated inside the ring, but do you want to test out that theory outside of it?"

"Time and place, Valentine," Jonas responded.

"Fellas, calm down," Christopher said. "There seems to be too much testosterone in this room. We all came here to try and come to an agreement. Let's continue down that path and not this other one." He always tried to be the voice of reason. Christopher glanced at Jaden. "There's nothing we can do about the Lotus Development now, son. Be easy as you young men put it."

That seemed to tickle Leslie as a chuckle slipped from his throat.

"The Fairburn development belongs to us," Christopher said matter of factly.

Xavier's brow arched. "That's your way of coming to an agreement?" Xavier said.

"That's what he said." This time it was Jonathon who'd spoken.

"That's not how negotiations work," Xavier continued, "And if I didn't know any better, I'd suspect you all didn't come here to work this out at all. So why waste our time? I'm sure we all have more important things to attend to instead of showing off which one of us has bigger balls."

"We all know who has bigger balls, X," Jonathon said, causing a round of laughter to roll from the Roses.

Xavier chuckled. "Oh yeah," Xavier said. "I dare you to place the highest bid on it; we could even let you pick the judge, guarantee you mine are bigger, baby boy."

"Fellas, this isn't getting us anywhere," Jordan said, finally inserting his voice.

Jonathon held daggers on Xavier, and Xavier puckered his lips and blew him a kiss. "Anytime," Xavier mouthed, tired of the shit show going on in the room. He'd rather be anywhere but here, but especially with Corinne. He flipped his wrist and checked the time. The last time he'd spoken with her she and Camilla were on their way to lunch, and if he could get out of here quick enough, he just might be able to catch her.

There was a knock on the door, and everyone turned their attention to it.

"Expecting company?" Kyle asked.

Christopher also checked the time. "No, any of you?"

Leslie glanced at his sons and they declined. "It doesn't appear so," Leslie said.

"Come in," Jonas barked.

The door opened, and London Jones tiptoed into the room. London was the part-time caregiver for Jaden's mother-in-law Adeline. She glanced around the modern executive space and was taken back by the fierce-looking gorgeous brothers in the room. She'd been privy to the charm of the Rose men for years now that she worked for them, but seeing them in the room with the Valentines brought all the sexiness in one place to a mind-screeching halt. She could barely remember why she entered. Her eyes traveled over Lance's braided locks and chocolate brown skin, but it was when her eyes fell on Kyle Valentine that a buzz hit the core of her body so hard she almost jumped out of her skin. *Oh, my damn,* she thought. *I have surely stepped into the Lion's Den.*

Chapter Ten

Kyle's lips spread into a sexy smile, and he winked then took an eye over London's complete form. London perused him right back, taking notice of his sharp haircut, designer shades that didn't hide his light brown eyes behind tint, and the milk chocolate skin he was designed in. Another crawling buzz skittered down her skin, and chills populated all over her body.

"London, is everything okay?" Jaden asked, rounding the table to stand in front of her, effectively cutting off her view from Kyle. London wondered if he'd done it on purpose but didn't have time to ponder on it since she'd left Adeline in the car.

"Yes… um, no," she said, thrown off her game. "Adeline has misplaced her keys, and I don't have mine, so neither of us can get in the house."

"Where is Adeline now?" Jaden asked.

"She's downstairs in the car waiting for me to come back. Should we wait for your meeting to be over? I didn't know if you'd want me to or not, and Claudia is still at S & M Financial."

"No, I'll give you my key. Just make sure to place it in the bowl in the foyer when you get home so you don't lose it."

"Yes, sir."

Jaden removed his keys and handed them over to London.

"Thank you, sorry for interrupting."

"No problem, see you later."

London left the room but not before sparing one last glance back at Kyle who still held a piercing eye on her parting form. Again, he winked, and London blushed then shuffled out the door.

When Kyle brought his attention back across the table, he was met with glares from all of the men except Christopher. Kyle chuckled.

"You guys should relax more often," he said. "I'd send you over my own personal masseuse if it would help you enjoy life more."

"We enjoy life just fine," Jonathon said.

"Let's wrap this up, shall we?" Xavier prompted.

Hunter spoke next. "This is the reality. We've both placed bids on the Fairburn development. I want it because my wife wants to start a charity with the three hotels in the development's district. It's important to her, and she's important to me. I'd like to give her the chain of hotels as a wedding gift." Hunter's gaze hopped to each of their faces. "Surely, you can understand the gift of giving, right? The need to have The Fairburn development is not a selfish one, so I'm inclined to ask you to drop your bid, so we can do right by the property." He paused again. "However, if you need an extra push, we're willing to make you part owner of the Lotus Development in return."

"Therein lies our problem, Hunter," Jonas spoke back. Hunter was tired of Jonas already; he liked to ruffle Hunter's feathers. "We want the housing development for charity as well. We plan to house victims of home invasions in that district. As you know, our mother was killed in a home invasion when we were adolescents. We're dedicating Fairburn to her legacy."

They all eyeballed each other.

"So, the bidding war continues then," Kyle said, summing it all up.

"If you don't want to hand it over, so be it," Jaden said.

Hunter exhaled harshly and shook his head.

"This is unfortunate," Leslie added.

"Yes, I would say so," Christopher responded.

The men waited another beat just to make sure neither of the families would bite.

"Okay, then," Xavier was the first to stand. "It was interesting catching up with you fellas." He rebuttoned his jacket. "Until we meet again."

Leslie stood next, along with Kyle and Lance. They filed out of the room one behind the other, leaving the Rose men looking after them with disdain.

———

"I can't believe I got you out of that apartment," Corinne said.

With a hair flip, Camilla waved down a waiter, and the women skipped over to their table. The light pink baby doll blouse Camilla wore fit snuggly around her bosom, uplifting them but flaring around her small pouch of a stomach. The top three buttons were unfastened, and a sterling silver necklace hung from her neck and disappeared between her cleavage.

"Hi, yes," Camilla began, "my friend and I have been sitting here twenty minutes, and no one has come to take our orders. Is everyone on a break or?"

"I'm so sorry," the woman responded. "I'm Alana. I can take your order."

"But will you be our waitress?"

"Yes, ma'am, I'm sorry. I did just come back from lunch."

"It would've been nice to know that ahead of time."

Camilla glanced at Corinne. "Do you know what you want?"

Corinne laughed. "Girl, that pregnancy must have you hungry as a horse because I've never seen you get an attitude over food."

"A horse has nothing on my appetite right now."

Corinne giggled and placed her order as did Camilla. The waitress apologized again then scurried away to place their order.

"Now back to what you were saying. Don't hate, I could never get enough of Hunter. He's like nobody I've ever known."

"Puts Steven to shame, huh?"

"Steven who?"

Corinne laughed. Steven was Camilla's ex-fiancé. After calling off their wedding, she'd had enough of him and uprooted her life in their hometown of Miami to take on the position as anchor for WTZB in Chicago. Soon after, she met Hunter, and everything from there was history.

"Exactly. Just for the record, I love this new hairdo," she said, pointing out Camilla's fresh bob.

"Oh, thank you, baby, it has to get transformed every other day because Hunter—"

"TMI!" Corinne screeched.

"Oh, sorry not sorry."

They laughed, and Camilla pointed out, "Yours looks good, too. When did you ever have time to get it done, and that's a new outfit."

Corinne smirked. "Don't pretend to act like you know what my wardrobe looks like," she joked.

"Oh, honey, please, I know a new fit when I see one, and that jumpsuit you're wearing is fresh off the rack and fire."

"It does fit my curves nicely, doesn't it?" Corinne asked, rising to her feet to pose left then right, sticking her hips out.

Camilla laughed and nodded. "It does."

The all white one-piece had been similar to the peach one she'd worn during her paragliding adventure with Xavier. Corinne had noticed the way Xavier stared down every inch of her womanly figure, and the locking of his jaw hadn't gone past her either. She reclaimed her seat.

"Maybe I was looking to get a little attention today." She flipped her shoulder-length hair, revealing diamond stud earrings that were attached to her lobes.

"Attention from who, I don't go both ways."

Corinne choked out a laugh, and Camilla joined in on her glee. When she calmed enough, Corinne responded.

"Don't act like you don't want all of this," she said, making a show of waving a hand down her body like Vanna White on Wheel of Fortune.

Camilla laughed again, and the waitress jogged to their table with their drinks.

"It will be about five minutes. I've put in a rush order."

"Thank you," they both chimed.

Camilla took a sip of her sweet tea then went back to their conversation but her phone rang stealing her attention.

"Hold on for a second," Corinne said rummaging through her purse. When she lifted the smartphone to her face, she blew out a frustrated breath and considered answering it but decided not to.

"Who was that?" Camilla asked gauging her reaction.

"Unknown Caller," she said waving it off. "It's the second time I've gotten that type of call and it's annoying."

"So which one of your ex-boyfriends is it?" Camilla teased.

Corinne shrugged her shoulders and teased back, "Who knows."

They laughed and returned to their conversation.

"You must've talked to Xavier to be bossed up and looking all sparkly and shit."

Corinne chuckled. "I always talk to him."

Camilla was delighted and intrigued as her brows rose in response. She exhaled and relaxed against her seat. "So, what's going on with you and Xavier?"

Corinne licked her lips, and her eyes closed for a hot second before reopening.

"That good, huh?" Camilla said.

"When you said you've never met anyone like Hunter, I have to say I understand."

Camilla nodded.

"We're dating," Corinne blurted.

"Dating as in officially a couple or just seeing where things go, or friends with benefits."

"All of that," Corinne said, "well except for the benefits part if you're talking about sex. That hasn't happened, but Xavier can't keep his lips off of me, and I can't deny him either."

Camilla was nodding again, and a smile cruised across her lips.

"I just want to thank you now for introducing us. Even if this doesn't turn out the way I hope, I still thank you for this experience."

Camilla giggled deeply. "My pleasure. Hey, you guys hit it off, and really you should thank Hunter. If he hadn't proposed and we hadn't double dated, you wouldn't have met Xavier."

"Well not at that moment, but with you guys engaged…"

"Right, you would've met him eventually, I see where you're going."

"Yeah, so thank you anyway, and thank Hunter for me."

Camilla laughed again.

"We're going to Africa."

Camilla's eyes bulged. "When?"

"Next week."

Camilla gasped. "Why?"

"I told him about the little girl I sponsored when I was young, and he asked me if I've ever been to Zambia before. The next thing I know, we were planning a trip."

"Oooh, now I think I'm jealous."

"Don't be, you can come with if you want. Trust me, Xavier and I would pay you and Hunter no mind."

They both laughed.

"I'm sure, but I couldn't get on a plane right now. The way my nausea is set up, I wouldn't be any fun."

Corinne pouted.

"Besides, I would need at least a month of a heads up to give WTZB."

"Oh please, who do you think you're fooling?"

"What are you talking about?"

"Camilla you've got WTZB wrapped around your fingers. Honey, you made your debut in Chicago, snagged one of the wealthiest bachelors off the market, became the face of WTZB, and have already been promoted, and you haven't been there 90 days. Who does that?"

Camilla wiggled her eyebrows and pointed to herself. "Me, that's who, I'm an all-around superwoman."

The women laughed louder, garnering the attention of

some nearby patrons. A few men in the restaurant winked over at them, and the ladies nodded back.

"How can you stand all of the attention?" Corinne asked.

"Honestly, I hardly notice it because when I'm with Hunter, the only thing I see is him. It's quite scary at times."

Corinne's smile dropped slightly. "What do you mean?"

"You said it yourself, he's one of Chicago's wealthiest bachelors. Women don't care, they will continue to throw themselves at him to see if he's game, and I'm so in love with him, Corinne. What happens if—"

"Oh no, we are not about to do that," Corinne interjected. Corinne sat upright from her slouched position and crossed her legs. "Do you really think Hunter would hurt you like that?"

Camilla's gaze wandered off for a brief second then she grimaced. When her eyesight returned to Corinne, a small smile cornered her lips. "No, he just seems too perfect you know."

Corinne did know. Thoughts of Monica's warning of Xavier were never too far from her mind. But the way Corinne saw it, she couldn't let that fear hinder her and possibly lose out on a lifetime of happiness or a month of happiness. However long the happiness lasted, she wanted to soak up every second of it.

"Look I get it, but, Camilla, don't you dare let anything come between you and Hunter. Especially those types of thoughts. They're the devil and meant to ruin your relationship."

"You're right." Camilla perked up and Corinne tapped the table with her hand.

"I know I am, now, let's have a conversation worth its weight in gold."

"Which would be?"

"Your wedding!"

This brought on another elaborate smile from Camilla. She sighed dreamily.

"It's in a month, Corinne said. "How will you ever get the whole shebang done in time?"

"Girl, Hunter has contacts, I mean the kinds that could reach out to the President of the United States. So, when I tell you it will go off without a hitch, believe me."

Corinne nodded. "Damn, a man with all the fixings. Must give you a toothache to be so freakin' sweet."

Camilla laughed with a nod. "I've got the feeling you'll find out soon."

That comment just about took Corinne's breath away.

"Girl, don't even play with me like that."

"Who's playing?"

"I could only dream."

"How does he treat you?"

"Like a princess."

"That'll change," Camilla said.

Corinne frowned. "What?"

"That'll change. Right now, he's treating you all delicate. Holding your hand, touching you gently, kissing you passionately. Am I right?"

Corinne's eyes roamed from side to side. "Yeah…" She was afraid of where this was going next.

"But then there are times when he clutches your body, like a grip here, a solid hold there, he might even growl just a bit but not too much to scare you away, am I getting warmer?"

Corinne swallowed. "Yeah…"

"It's because he's really kin to a rare species; one that's protective, possessive, dominant, and animalistic. He'll treat you like a princess now, but once you two mate…"

"Did you really just say mate?"

Camilla nodded. "He's a rare breed, and after the sex, you'll go from princess to Queen status. Not that you're not a Queen now, but you get the idea. Then, not only will he continue to be the way he is now, but it will come with a little extra funk. A kick that will re-work your entire galaxy." Corinne nodded. "Trust me, I know what I'm talking about."

Corinne's heart raced, and a ruckus at the entrance of the restaurant pulled her and Camilla's attention.

"Don't look now, but something wicked this way comes…" Camilla crooned.

Corinne did turn to look, and the splendor of Xavier and Hunter strolling side by side made her pussy thump so hard Corinne thought she would have an orgasm where she sat.

"Damn, they fine as hell," Corinne said.

Camilla sucked in her lips. "The both of them," she agreed and wasn't mad for a second that Corinne noticed Hunter's gorgeousness.

The sway in their walk was confident, prevailing, and supreme. Corinne and Camilla could practically see the women fall to their feet as the men made a beeline for their table.

"And their all ours," Camilla said, lifting her hand to the side for a secret smack. Corinne met her halfway but couldn't respond as Xavier's bravado had completely made her mute.

Chapter Eleven

The month indicated it was springtime, but the weather some days was hot then cold. However, Corinne watching Xavier stroll up on her liquified her flesh right down to her bones. It was obvious that he'd just come from a meeting since he was dressed down in an all-white Brioni suit, tailored and spruced over his expansive shoulders. A purple tie was tucked neatly inside his jacket and a purple pocket square perched out of the jacket's top pocket. He was a snack that was about to turn into Corinne's whole entrée, and he didn't even know it.

When the men pulled up on them, debonair smiles laced their lips, further causing the women to tighten their thighs.

"Is their room for two more?" Xavier asked, staring down at Corinne.

"Waiter!" Corinne snapped her fingers, and Camilla fell

out laughing. "We need chairs over here, where's the damn waiter when you need one!"

The men chuckled and found their own chairs. They both got comfortable next to their women, bringing a spicy scent with them. Corinne couldn't help but take in the way Xavier's trousers lifted just barely as he sat, showing his brown oiled ankles and white oxford shoes. Her eyes drifted up his strong thighs to the way the material huddled around his crotch. The material jerked, causing Corinne to jerk with it. She covered her chest with a hand. *Oh my God*.

"If you keep staring at him, he'll continue to leap until you calm him down," Xavier's thick voice strummed.

Corinne's nipples hardened, and her gaze shifted from his pelvis to his beautiful angled face. A blush rose to her cheeks, more so because of the brazen nature that affected her. She instantly fell into a lure, and her actions followed her body's commands.

"You know, I've always wanted to wrap your beard around my fingers like this," she said, raveling the threads around her fingers, "and pull you to my lips, like this," she continued, dragging his face to hers. Their lips connected, and the force of the mesh sent a jolting sting through them both. For a second, they stared at one another, a searing heat flashing between them. The next second, Xavier opened her mouth with the blunt force of his tongue and sucked the taste buds on her palate.

"Mmmm," Corinne moaned. Her eyes closed, and she didn't see it but felt his strong hand slip up her thigh to grip her around the inner edges where her thigh and vagina met.

Not once did her conscious tell her to *stop* or *no* or *this is inappropriate.*

With the tip of his pointing finger, Xavier circled the outer seams of her pussy right where her clitoris sat underneath the garment while the rest of his hand squeezed tightly against her thigh. A thud thumped from her panties as the invigorating titillation coursed through her. Simultaneously, she yelped in his mouth, and he swallowed the breath she released.

"Excuse me," the waitress hesitated, unsure if she should proceed.

Xavier and Corinne took their time pulling apart. When they did, Corinne glanced over at the hovering waitress as Xavier kept his poignant gaze on Corinne's lips.

"Your food, ma'am," the waitress said, placing the plate in front of her.

"Thank you," Corinne's husky voice throttled. She cleared her throat, recognizing the sultriness in her tone.

"You're welcome, can I get your dates anything?"

"Yes…" Xavier's voice drawled. "A bowl of strawberries." His gaze never left Corinne's face.

Corinne's nipples were so hard she was sure they'd receded into her breasts.

"I've got strawberries," she said.

Xavier glanced down at her plate, his eyes drunk with lust. "Great minds," he said. His grizzly tone made her quiver, and she watched as his manicured fingers reached for the fruit and pierced off the stem.

"This is a big piece of fruit," he said. "How wide can you open your mouth, Bella Anima?" He sat the end of the strawberry in the cove of his mouth, and Corinne leaned into him, covering the butt of the berry with hers. Sucking in, the heat from his mouth tingled her upper lip just as she crushed the fruit with her teeth. Juice spilled down into the corner of her lips, and Xavier hungrily licked every remnant that remained.

"Ahem," someone cleared their throat, but Xavier was too busy devouring Corinne's mouth to notice.

"They will order in a second," Camilla said from the other side of the table, eyes wide and mouth hanging at the open way Xavier and Corinne made out.

"No worries," the waitress said her eyes also wide. "I'll be back momentarily."

"We won't be ready in a moment..." Xavier eased out. His engine was running high, hot, and on overload. He'd wanted Corinne in so many ways that he struggled to calm down much less stop himself. Without hesitation, his other hand connected with her other thigh and with Zeus-like strength, he lifted her, then shifted her as his grip rounded to the back and held firmly under the crease of her ass.

Surprised by the macho movement, Corinne's foot lifted and the chair she once occupied flipped over. She squealed as Xavier planted her on his lap. Her hands clutched his shoulder to steady herself as her legs dangled over the sides of his powerful thighs. The lurching of his dick waved across the seat of her pants, sending a riveting cauldron of heat attacking her core.

"Oh my God," Camilla said. She wasn't ashamed that she'd been suddenly turned on watching the two. *This must be what porn is like for couples*, she thought.

Xavier recaptured Corinne's mouth, and snapshots from camera phones burst as patrons took pictures of Xavier and Corinne in the risqué position. He sucked her tongue and closed his entire mouth around hers in an uninhibited urgency to taste her thoroughly. The pair could hear nothing but their kisses and sucks and groans. See nothing but one another. No one and nothing mattered to them until…

"Brother…"

Hearing Hunter's voice knocked reality back into Xavier, and slowly with disinclination, he pulled off of Corinne's lips but not before his tongue drug across the ceiling of her mouth. He sucked her lips as his tongue exited and nibbled down her mouth to her jaw.

Corinne was breathing hard as hell. She could hardly maintain a sense of sanity after the way he'd just consumed her. More importantly, if he'd made her feel like this with their clothes on, then what the hell would it be like when they finally made love?

Xavier peered at her before taking a glance around the restaurant. Wide open gawked smiles were on people's faces, and this would no doubt be the center of the news tomorrow.

"I should be embarrassed," Xavier said, his gaze penetrating directly through Corinne's eyes, "but I'm not. I can't apologize for this."

Corinne's breath was still bated, her chest rising and falling.

"Um…" she looked around, discombobulated. "We're

matching," she said, thinking of the only thing that came to mind at the moment.

Xavier cocked his head and smiled lazily as he took an all-pervading eye over her white jumpsuit. "So, we are," he said.

"I should probably get up." But she didn't move; instead, she stared Xavier off, wondering if it would be okay to drag him off to the nearest restroom and throw caution to the unruly wind that tumbled inside her.

Xavier leaned to the side and lifted her chair with one hand, propping it back at his side with no wiggle room for Corinne to be too far away.

"Let me help you," he said, placing another firm grip on her thighs.

Corinne rose from his lap and found her way back into her chair. As she relaxed against her seat, she crossed her legs and fought inwardly to calm her racing heart.

"Okay, now that we've gotten that full show out of the way," Camilla said with a smirk, "maybe we can eat. I'm starving here."

Xavier readjusted his tie, although it didn't need it. His hunger for Corinne was still preeminent, and it was taking extreme focus to behave. He tried to alter his thoughts by changing the topic.

"Brother," Xavier began, "I told Corinne about our b-boy band back in junior high and college."

"You didn't," Hunter said.

Xavier chuckled. "Yes, I did, and she wants a performance from us for her and Camilla."

"A b-boy band?" Camilla said loudly, glancing at Corinne. "Why am I just now hearing about this?"

Still stuck, Corinne blinked rapidly then glanced around the table. "Hmm?"

Camilla snapped her fingers. "Earth to Corinne."

Xavier examined her closely. "Are you all right?" His thick voice cruised.

Corinne cleared her throat but didn't speak only handed over a nod. If she had to be honest, hell no she wasn't all right. She was completely out of sorts, and her fingers were itching to slip back into her panties again. Why the hell did Xavier have to be so damn irresistible? She made up her mind the next time they were alone it was going down, she didn't give a damn if they were sitting in the middle of traffic.

She rolled her tongue over her gums then finally found her vocals.

"You should ask Hunter," she said. "Why hasn't he told you?"

Camilla glanced at Hunter. "Yeah, why haven't you told me?"

"It isn't something that's come up, Angel."

"Hmph," Camilla said. "So who was all in this band, and did you have songs or what?"

"Only four of us were in the band. Raphael didn't like the spotlight. He abhorred it. So he was our writer, and Kyle was like our manager. He booked the shows and handled paperwork. We all play a different instrument, but they weren't all necessary when we performed. It just depended on the song."

"So when will I get this performance, huh?"

"We," Corinne interjected. "When will WE get this performance."

Xavier and Hunter chuckled.

"I think our reception is as good a time as any, what do you think?" Hunter asked Camilla.

"I think it's perfect," she said dreamily. Hunter leaned in and kissed her lips.

"I love you," he said.

"I love you, too."

Corinne's mind conjured images of she and Xavier speaking those words, and it sent a wave down her body that snagged her breath. When his warm hand reached out to cover hers underneath the table, she glanced at him, and he winked, knocking her nerves further into turmoil.

Chapter Twelve

The last seven days had felt like three, and that was surprising since whenever Corinne was looking forward to something it usually took forever to come to pass. Nevertheless, she and Xavier were on their way to Zambia, Africa, and the excitement she felt was extraordinary.

"Do you have your passport?" Xavier asked, glancing from the newspaper he'd been studying for the last fifteen minutes.

"Of course, I always have my passport. It's attached to my hip like most people's cell phones."

Xavier chuckled. They were on board his Boeing 747 VIP private jet halfway to the motherland.

"Perfect," he said.

"It would've been a shame had I forgotten it since it's too late to turn back now."

"We could always get you a Visa, so either way we're getting into the country."

"Do you have connections with everyone?"

Xavier thought about it for a moment. "Not quite. Depends. I'm not a fan of Ireland, but if I need to visit I could always…"

Corinne was shaking her head.

"What?" he asked.

"The fact that you could get the connection if you needed a connection just means you have connections."

Xavier grinned. "You've got me there."

Corinne's smile barely lifted as her eyes roamed over Xavier's attire. He was comfortable in a crew neck white shirt and khaki cargo shorts. On his feet a pair of open toe sandals, and his toes were clearly pedicured and oiled from the shine they held. Monica's words came back to haunt her again, so she couldn't stop herself from asking the inevitable question.

"Does it bother you that there's a certain expectation set in the eyes of the media about you when it comes to the opposite sex?"

Xavier glanced up from his newspaper then folded it and tucked it away in a compartment attached to the chair he sat in.

"A certain expectation?"

"Yeah, you know, they've pinned you to be this Casanova who sees women as items that you can use then dispose of at your will."

Xavier glanced around then back to Corinne. "Did I

miss a morning report or something, should I turn on the news?"

Corinne chuckled. "No, nothing like that." She paused then glanced away for an extended period, hesitant to continue down this conversational road. Truth was, she was slowly falling for him, and even after the brave front she put up with Camilla, Corinne worried that maybe she shouldn't be.

"What are you really asking me, Bella?"

Corinne swiped her tongue across her teeth then turned her gaze back to him.

"Are you a frequent flyer of the mile-high club?"

"Am I..." Xavier's words paused, and a smile registered across his resplendent mouth. He saw the seriousness in her face, and the smile faded. "No," he said. "But you think I am."

Corinne pursed her lips and swallowed. "I've heard a thing or two."

"And it bothers you."

"I— I just thought I'd ask, it's no big deal."

He moved from his seated position; his slow stroll predatory and indicative of how his thoughts processed as he closed in. He reached for her hand and tugged, and Corinne stood to her feet.

"Do you want what the media thinks, or do you want the truth," he asked.

Corinne's heart knocked against her breastbone. "I want the truth." She gazed at him.

"Okay... the truth is, I've had a sexual attraction to you since the very moment I laid eyes on you." His hands slid down her waist and wrapped around her back. "More than that, there's been this unnatural chemistry surrounding us that's made me want you in ways that a man should only want his wife." His palm settled in the center of her back and he pushed her closer, sealing them in an embrace so tight one couldn't breathe without the other's permission. "Your aura drives me crazy, and I act without thinking often like in the restaurant last week.

"That would've never happened before you, Bella. There's no media station or newspaper that has caught me in such an awkward position before. I'll tell you why. I don't usually trust women. I've found that they can be manipulative and conniving to the point where they are toxic. So, part of the media's representation of me holds some truth. I have been seen with various women. It does depict me as a womanizer. But the honest to God truth is, none of those women can say they've had the pleasure of knowing me intimately. Because I never gave any of them a chance to. They were merely a means to an end. A date for an event.

"Was I attracted to any of them? Sure. But I'm a very selective man, Bella Anima, and I respect women, so they'll never catch a scandal about me in the news. If you hadn't noticed, I'm a workaholic. Over the years, I've trained myself to be this way because any woman that I bed means more to me than a mere romp in the sack for the sake of satisfying my flesh, and I would like to believe that holds true with the woman I'm with."

They stared each other off, and Xavier could tell she wanted to believe him but saw her internal struggle.

"Ask me?" he said, knowing there was more.

"Nadine Benson."

Hearing Nadine's name come from Corinne's lips didn't surprise him like he thought it would. In his heart, Xavier knew it was only a matter of time before the topic of their previous relationship resurfaced. Especially, since Nadine had recently brought the possibility of their relationship's revival back to the spotlight. He locked his jaw then sighed.

"What about her?" His voice was calm and deep.

"Who is she to you?"

He stared her off for a long second. "She is no one."

Corinne saw the way his face locked and the semi-frostiness in his response. That indicated that she was... someone.

"Would you lie to me, Xavier?"

Xavier broke eye contact with her, and Corinne was desperate to find it again. She could see the truth in his eyes. She could see every emotion displayed in his eyes. When he reconnected, she refused to lose it again.

"I have no reason to lie to you, Bella. She was someone important. That was long ago. It's been over between us for almost three years." His hand found her chin. "I'm only seeing you." He paused. "I only want you."

Corinne's heart knocked. She believed him, and a rushing breath escaped her as if she'd been holding on to it. It was true, Corinne had seen a repeat of the episode with Nadine hinting at a reconnection with Xavier, and Corinne wanted to know if Nadine had a dog in this fight. Xavier cocked his head to the side, and he asked what she'd been thinking.

"Do you believe me?"

Corinne felt so many emotions at that moment she could hardly respond fast enough.

"I need to know that you believe me, Bella Anima. It's important for us in order to move forward."

"Yes," she said. "I believe you."

A smile tugged at his lips, and he caressed her chin. Corinne couldn't explain the jubilation that consumed her. It was like a happiness that she never knew existed. Xavier was the real deal, and she believed it now without a doubt.

"Make love to me, Xavier."

His arm tightened around her waist at her request.

"Corinne…"

"Don't make me beg," she said. She wiggled out of his embrace, and her feet backpedaled slowly, one behind the other. "I want you." Her fingers skipped up her dress, and her hands reached behind her back to unclasp the three top buttons. "I need you." Reaching below her hem, she lifted the featherweight gown over her head and let it fall off of her arms to the floor. "You said you usually don't trust women," she went on, "but you trust me, right?"

Xavier completely froze, and his eyes went dark as night. His gaze outlined her frame, taking in the see-through white laced bra that teased him with the distention of her dark brown nipples. His eyes blazed down her skin to the thin-strapped panties that curved her hips and squeezed out her bodacious thighs. Corinne's hands cruised across her breasts, and with a snap, the front clasp was undone.

When Xavier took her, he did it quickly. Before Corinne had a chance to bat an eyelid, she was in Xavier's arms. Her legs encircled his waist, and she tugged and snatched at his shirt. They succeeded in getting it over his head, but it jammed around his thick neck and toned biceps, refusing to be discarded, exposing his chiseled abs. Corinne's fingers skipped down the ridges in his chest and dived down to his shorts. She scrambled to get them unfastened, but when she did, Xavier hauled her up and removed them from his toned hips effortlessly.

She didn't witness him remove the condom, but she saw him rip the gold package with his teeth. With one hand, he reached for her thong and snatched the string from her body. The material was disposed of with a quick yank, and the head of his dick skated across her heated cavern with a deliberately prolonged dig. Corinne trembled, and a moan escaped her lips.

"Yes," he said. "I trust you." He shifted and rolled the magnum down his extended shaft. "But the question is, do you trust me, Bella?"

Xavier's voice was profound, and his mouth floated above Corinne's ear with their chests compressed. His lips brushed her temples, distributing a kiss there so affectionate that it dissolved her further. He trailed to her lips and hovered there, waiting for her answer.

"Yes," she whispered against his mouth, burning for his undertaking.

Desire built within them, and when Xavier entered Corinne, her back bowed, and her spine contracted at the force of his blunt entry.

"Oh my God!"

Corinne was consumed with each edge of his wide-reaching cock, and it spread her pussy inch by excruciating inch.

"Aaaaaah…" she sang, her head falling back, and her mouth stuck on O.

Her hands held a firm grip on his shoulders, her nails sinking into his skin. Xavier filled her fully, burying himself to the hilt. A blaze of heat spiral through Corinne's body, and her intake of breath was so sharp she almost choked on it. She exhaled.

"Oh… my God," and her toes curled. Corinne didn't know what she expected, but the thoroughness of his drilling, and slapping against her ass was mind-bending.

He kissed the side of her face while his hips rocked in and out viciously. She held on to him as if letting him go would cause her to combust into a million tiny embers. The heat that covered their skin became a blanket of instant perspiration, and their breathing kicked into gear as did their bump and grind.

"Xavier…" she purred. "Baby, oh my God."

Xavier's strokes became forceful as his hips dipped and tunneled inside her womb. Slaps of diffusion from their connection penetrated the aircraft, and a thunderous sound, something like a growl trekked from Xavier's lips.

"Fuuuu-ck, girl!"

His mouth discovered her neck, trailing down her shoulders as their rocking became hedonistic. He licked down her breasts and sucked in a nipple sharp and heavy, causing Corinne's body to arch more into him. Concurrently, Xavier slammed into her bottom, holding her derriere while feasting on her breasts.

Corinne screamed and held on for dear life while Xavier found pleasure in consuming her whole. They filled themselves with one another, completely immersed in their joining.

"Oh my God… baaaaby!" she screamed, clutching his shoulders as he clenched her ass while thrusting so ferociously hard that a shockwave tore through her abdomen and caused her legs to spasm. "Aaaaaah!"

Xavier stood on his feet with no barrier or furniture to bare the force of their endeavor. It was all them, grinding and bouncing against each other in a fervent ecstasy that shot them higher than any aircraft could.

They embraced tightly and kissed each other so hard it hurt. With their hearts slamming together and their libidos at an all-time high, Xavier and Corinne disintegrated into one another, enthralled in their passionate coupling. Minutes turned into hours that they joined, switched positions, and flexed as if they were in a sexual yoga class. When they came, it was together. Corinne's legs quaked, and she tightened her thighs, tossing her head back as a whale of a scream ripped through her existence.

"I'm coming, baby, oh my God!"

Now on top of her on the floor, Xavier sucked in her tongue and pounded her pussy with such strength she was sure he was trying to find a place of residence.

"Come with me, Bella," he said, biting down on her neck, his teeth piercing her flesh, causing her orgasm to squirt in intervals of cream.

Her body jerked repetitively, and Corinne was speechless. Her mouth hung open, but no sound came out because it had been ripped from her being. Only choked air cut from her lungs as if she was gasping for oxygen.

"Grrrrrrr fuuuuu-ck!" Xavier barked as he too shot a load of cum inside her. His lips fell to her ear, and their breathing labored as they both twitched, and their ears popped while they continued their release.

"I... I..." Corinne said, trying to construct an intelligible sentence. "Oh, fuck it," she said, passing out in his arms.

Chapter Thirteen

*H*is immediate response was of worry and his reaction was to check her pulse. It was beating as rapidly as his heart, and Xavier breathed a sigh of relief then realized she'd been beaten into uber submission. *That was a first,* he thought but didn't deny that it gave him a real ego boost. As if he needed it. Removing himself from her sanctuary, Xavier lifted her and carried Corinne to the bedroom in the rear of the aircraft. Laying her down, he pulled the covers back and readjusted them both, deciding to lay with her for a minute before showering.

That instant gratification had been worth the agonizing wait, but he wasn't done with Corinne by far. He'd give her time to readjust then take her as frequently as she could stand it. The uninhibited way she'd given herself over to him, undressing and pleading with him to indulge in what they both wanted lit a fire so hot within him it was useless to fight it, and he was glad he didn't.

It wasn't long before Xavier joined Corinne in dreamland. Together, they rested, spooned underneath each other, sleeping like neither of them had slept in years. Their dreams were similar, with Xavier finding himself on bended knee, and Corinne seeing herself in a wedding gown so beautiful it brought tears to her parents' eyes. She was the first one to wake from rest, and when she did, the warmth that surrounded her drew her closer than before. Her eyes fluttered, and they traveled up his sculpted chest and his thick throat. His natural scent cuddled her, holding Corinne hostage in the cove of his embrace.

They were naked. It appeared that Xavier had finally gotten rid of the shirt that was jammed around his neck. His skin was silky smooth like a chocolate Milky Way. Her mind traveled to her dream, and the thoughts she'd entertained about being his wife. She understood completely the way Camilla felt. How often was it you found a man that wasn't thrilled by the thought of meaningless sex? One who kept his priorities in line and respected women as if it was a true passion of his. Corinne couldn't speak for all women, but there was the saying that the way a man treated his mother would be the ultimate way he would treat his woman.

Corinne had yet to meet Xavier's parents, but if he was a reflection of them, then she could rest assured that they'd done a fabulous job fashioning their son. Thinking about his parents made Corinne think about hers. She hadn't spoken with Brenda and Daniel Thomas since last Saturday, and she was sure her father was waiting for her weekly call.

Corinne shifted in an attempt to pull from Xavier's embrace. She could sneak off to the bathroom and have a quick conversation with her parents then hopefully sneak back in bed and cuddle with Xavier until they arrived in Africa.

However, when Corinne attempted another shift, Xavier's arms tightened around her, and his snake of a dick pushed into her abdomen, causing immediate arousal to tread to her pussy. *Oh shit.* Her eyes fluttered to his face, but he was still sleeping soundly. Feeling carefree, Corinne placed her mouth against his throat and kissed his hot skin. Her leg lifted, and her thigh clamped around his waist. His eyes fluttered just as Corinne brought kisses to the corner of his mouth.

He turned his face toward her just enough to settle his warm lips against hers. His eyes were mere slits, and his body brimmed with sexual awareness. Neither of them said a word as their lips mingled and their bodies tingled with new sensual chemistry. Corinne's hands slid up his solid chest, and she lifted, suspended just slightly in the air as she rolled him onto his back.

"Say you have another condom," she purred against his lips.

Xavier reached to the side and fumbled with a tray next to the bed that yielded another gold package. Corinne's eyes twinkled with delight, and she removed the package from his hand as she ground slowly on top of his enlarged erection.

"Mmmm," she moaned, watching Xavier watch her beneath the undertow of his dark gaze.

"What are you doing to me, woman?" he asked, his

voice holding an edgy depth. She continued to grind, coaxing her wetness all over his shaft with the condom still in her hand.

She shuddered. "You feel so good," she said. "So damn good."

Just the sheer friction from his hardness against her soft folds made them both shiver. The tantalizing tingles spread throughout their loins, seizing them both with a grand cover of heat. His hands reached for her waist and slid over her hips to grip her thighs.

"I love this skin you're in," he murmured, his voice a dark drum. "So soft, sweet, and beautiful."

"Mmmm, and I love… she lifted then and slid down his body, kissing his rock-hard chest and taking her tongue over the ridges in his creation. When she was faced with his dick, Corinne moaned before she could get the head of his arousal on her tongue, knowing it would be a meal she would never forget.

Her mouth wrapped around his flesh, and she opened her throat completely, taking in his inches like she'd been preparing for this moment her whole life.

A sharp intake of breath cut from Xavier's throat, and a wicked animalistic sound beat from the depths of his soul.

"Mmmm," Corinne said, completely turned on by the sweet taste of her cream mixed with the hardened length of his dick. She exercised her neck, sucking and slurping, bobbing and nodding on his cock with such intense satisfaction that she could feel her own orgasm gaining momentum.

"Fuck!" Xavier yelled. He lifted to his elbows then with one hand reached for her head and slipped his fingers in her tresses, where he took control of her plight and fucked her mouth. "Damn it, girl!" he growled coated in a smoldering heat with each thrust of his hips and each plunge down her throat.

He was out of control and had never come as quick from fellatio as he was about to come now. A deep detrimental sound trekked from his throat, and Xavier pulled her mouth off when he was at his wit's end. It was no use. Corinne could tell he was coming, and she wanted it all so she fought against his bravado, groveling for his dick to finish her supper efficiently.

"Corinne…" he barked, a single warning.

"Mmmm," Corinne moaned, taking him back into her mouth, and he ejaculated against the cavern of her throat.

Xavier bit down on his teeth, locking his jaw as a spiral of conjoined nerves tingled his balls and shot to the head of his cock.

"Fuck, fuck, fuck!" he shouted.

"Mmhmm," Corinne said, taking on every last drop he had to offer.

His breath was bated and as if Corinne knew there was nothing left she sucked off his head, her lips smacking in a loud POP. She peered up at him and met his hungry gaze, and his lips were lifted, and his teeth bared like a wild animal.

She should've expected his response, but she didn't, and by the time she knew what was happening, it was too late to run. He scooped her up, and she was on her back in seconds of her next breath. His lips were on her neck, her chest, her breasts, sucking in an areola then devouring her full bosom.

"Aaaah," she sucked in a mountain of air, with her mouth open and her head thrown back. His hot mouth trailed down her flat bare belly, and his tongue licked around the outie of her navel. He traveled beneath and sank his nose into her pussy. Her fragrance sent his nerves into complete disarray, and his tongue peeled open her flesh and traveled down her labia to sink inside her core.

"Oh my God!"

Her eyes widened, and her mouth was stuck, and her thighs shook. Xavier's tongue was limber, waving against the inside of her walls like he wanted a taste of her uterus.

"What the fuck…" she groveled, torn apart by the waylay of his tongue fucking her pussy. He stayed there for so long Corinne's body was in a constant state of shock, stiff and rigid, knowing his next move would be her undoing. And it was. When he removed his tongue, he punctured his way up her folds with it and like a wicked drill, pounded her clitoris so hard she came instantly.

"Aaaaaah!"

Her body seized, and her nerves unraveled. His entire mouth closed around her bud as he sucked, licked and pressurized his tongue against her sensitive flesh. The tingles that fled through her body kept her frozen and her toes curled so tight she was sure to catch a cramp at any second.

"Xavier!" she screamed. "Pa- please!"

A growl trekked from his throat. He was unrelenting, trying to eat her whole where there would be nothing left for anyone else. Her bottom fell out, and she came so hard that her body bounced in a temerarious tremble that shook her core and confused her mind.

Xavier opened his mouth wider, running his tongue back down her pussy to catch every sweet juice she released. Another growl escaped him, and he burped then laughed a deep profound sound without breaking from her sliding eruption of cream. He never let up, and Corinne clamped his head between her legs and screamed and screamed and screamed.

"Please!" she begged, needing to get away from him before she had a heart attack.

When Xavier slurped her last drop, he lifted his feral gaze to her and licked his wet mouth.

"That was the best damn meal I've ever had. How about you?"

Before she could respond, Corinne's eyes rolled, and she passed out again.

Chapter Fourteen

The smooth sounds of Prince's "The Most Beautiful Girl in the World" wrapped around the drum in Corinne's ear. Her eyes fluttered open, and her mouth parted on a smile. It wasn't the actual song, but Xavier's deep humming voice that serenaded her with the lyrics. He was singing to her and trailing a finger down the outline of her ear, neck, and shoulders.

"We're here, Bella Anima. Zambia awaits."

Corinne stretched. Her limbs flexed like that of a cat but went right back limp when it was over.

"I have on a shirt," she pointed out.

"You don't remember putting it on?"

"Hmmm, no. Did you help me?"

"Yeah."

"Why?"

"You shivered a few times after I got up."

"How do you know I shivered if you were gone?"

Xavier was quiet for a moment then he smirked.

"Because I've been watching you."

Corinne smiled. "Normally, that would creep me out, but no, it doesn't."

Xavier laughed. "That puts me at ease. I like watching you sleep. You're an angel."

Corinne smirked. "Then that would make you an angel, too. My guardian angel watching over me."

"I like the sound of that."

Corinne's smile held. "My body feels so light," she said.

Xavier chuckled. "That's because you've been emptied, love."

Corinne had to agree.

"I have a warm bubble bath waiting for you. There's no rush. We're here for three days, so take your time."

Corinne moaned and stretched again. "I'm sorry I couldn't take off four. I know that's what we originally planned."

"That's not a problem. We will make these three days count." He paused, and she removed her face from his neck and stared up at him.

"What," she asked, watching his eyes comb over her.

"You are the most beautiful girl in the world."

Corinne blushed. "You're just saying that because I sucked your soul from your body," she teased. It brought a rambunctious guffaw from Xavier as his smile spread in a beautiful pearly display.

"Yes," he admitted, "you did, but that is just icing on the

proverbial cake." He leaned down and kissed her lips, then her forehead, then her chin.

It was then that Corinne caught her first real look at him. He was fully dressed, and the spicy shower gel he'd used was coated on his skin.

"I'm holding us back, aren't I?"

"Not at all. We're on vacation. We'll do what we want. If you would like to linger another day, we will, but I won't promise to keep my hands to myself now that you've awakened the beast in me."

The thought of another round of sexual bliss with Xavier heightened her body but also reminded her of the soreness between her thighs.

"I'm up," she said, rising quickly.

He chuckled, and Corinne stood to her feet.

"Whoa," she said, pausing and reaching out for the wall.

Xavier was at her side. "Careful, Bella Anima, maybe you should lie back down."

Corinne steadied herself as the dizziness moved past her. "I'm good," she said.

"Sure?"

She smiled. "Yeah."

He pulled her close, bringing a glaze of heat as he kissed her lips. She felt so cozy with him she could live in that moment forever. She closed her eyes and inhaled then exhaled.

"Let me show you to the bathroom," he said, taking her hand and linking their fingers.

She followed him through the spacious design of the luxury aircraft to the bathroom that boasted hardwood floors and a clawfoot tub. Rose petals led a path to the bathtub and more petals floated on top of an arrangement of bubbles. Around the outer edges, tealight candles were lit and a vanilla fragrance wafted from the room.

Corinne glanced up at him. "For me?"

Xavier pulled her close again to kiss her lips. "Who else would it be for?"

Corinne blushed; she could get used to being taken care of like this.

"I'll tell you one thing, if you spoil me like this who knows when you'll get rid of me." She smirked.

"In that case, prepare to be showered."

Corinne smirked and strode away from him. As she sauntered, she reached for the top button of his shirt that she wore and unclasped them one by one keeping her back to him.

"I'll give you some privacy."

But before he could escape, Corinne spun around with the shirt falling from her fingers. It fell in a pool around her feet and soaked up the dangerous gaze Xavier wrapped her with. Her body shuddered as she thought of the things his mouth had done to her, the way he tasted every plane on her body. Xavier, on the other hand, was hard as a rock.

"Are you sure you don't want to bathe with me?" She turned her back to him and lifted her leg, deliberately sticking out her ass and giving him a peek of her mound.

"I'm sure If I get in there with you, we will spend the day on this jet." Xavier's voice was rough, and he was trying like all hell not to rush her. Unfortunately, his resolve was broken when Corinne stepped in the tub and dipped her body in the water then stood back to her feet.

Wet bubbles slid down her form, coasting over her brown skin, dark areolas, flat belly, and apex of her center.

"Fuck it," he said, removing his clothes piece by piece.

He'd already been in the shower, but it wouldn't hurt to clean up again after getting dirty one more time. He scooped her up in his arms, and Corinne laughed out loud then moaned once her legs wrapped around his waist and connected with his ridged shaft.

"Uuuuuh…" She threw her head back, and they made love throughout the afternoon.

XAVIER AND CORINNE WERE ABLE TO SALVAGE SOME PART of their day. Although it was late evening, the sun was still high in Zambia, and they took advantage, being met with a hatch-top safari vehicle. The heat index was sweltering with high humidity and the normal subtropical wet-dry atmosphere. But they were none the wiser as they sat comfortably leaned into one another as the cart drove over the rugged terrains.

"What do you think we'll see today?" Corinne asked.

Xavier was spaced out, and Corinne peered at him then asked another question.

"Hey, where are you?"

Xavier glanced down at her. "I'm here with you."

Corinne twisted her lips. "For a second you were gone. Where'd you go?"

Xavier's gaze flipped back to the road in front of them when he spoke.

"My family is in a bidding war with the Rose's over The Fairburn Development. It's going to get nasty before it's resolved." He sighed.

"How important is it to your family to have?"

The cart rocked slightly as they rode over a rough patch of terrain.

"Can you keep a secret?" He asked.

"Yeah."

Xavier licked his lips. "Hunter wants to gift the property to Camilla as a wedding gift. I'm sure you're aware that Camilla wants to start her charity by housing the homeless in the hotels."

Corinne's eyes widened and she nodded.

"Wow, that's incredible of Hunter to do."

"Yeah, but he may not get it."

Corinne frowned. "If you think that then you've already lost," she concluded.

Xavier smirked then leaned down placing a fiery kiss against her cheek.

"You're right. Thank you for reminding me." He paused. "Enough about business. You asked about the animals we might encounter. I'm thinking, maybe a few lions or elephants. Should we ask?"

"Oh." She smiled. "I didn't think you heard me."

"I always hear you," he said holding her with a steady gaze. "Excuse me, sir," Xavier called to their driver Phillip.

"How can I help you?" Phillip returned, his accent thick and deep-rooted.

"My lady would like to know which animals we might see today. Have any idea?"

"Oh, yes," Phillip said with a wide smile. "There will be, giraffes, lions, and surely elephants."

Xavier wiggled his brows at Corinne with a jaunty smile and an "I told you so" expression in his eyes. Corinne laughed and slapped his chest with a playful tap.

"However," Phillip continued, "if you're really adventurous, you could ride the elephant."

Corinne's eyes widened.

"Would you like that, Bella?"

"Is it safe?"

"Perfectly," Phillip responded.

"No, I mean for the elephant," Corinne said. "I've heard a thing or two about the dangers of riding their backs. I don't want to ride for the sake of my own selfish reasons if it's unethical to the animal."

Xavier stared at her in shocked silence but truly, he shouldn't have been surprised. He knew Corinne was a caring person. It was her personality trait that made him love her that much more.

"Elephant trails with our company are limited to thirty minutes tops. It's usually around one field and only so you can have the experience of seeing the land from up high," Phillip responded. "Our elephants are well taken care of, and we would not put them in harm's way for anyone, or anything."

Corinne bit the corner of her lips, pondering Phillip's words.

"I'll tell you what. My assistant and I will help you two

on top, and if it makes you feel better, you don't have to move, just sit for a second and take it all in."

Xavier studied her. "What do you think?"

"Hmmm, maybe."

Xavier pinched her chin. "All right Phillip, we're game."

Chapter Fifteen

"Oh my God!" Corinne squealed.

The green land stretched for miles around them. Wildlife, diverse and uncaged, trotted comfortably about creating a scene of paradise unlike anything Corinne had witnessed in the states.

"You said lions and elephants! This is…" she shook her head in disbelief. "Amazing."

They were perched on the back of a mother elephant with Xavier's arms wrapped around her waist. Antelope galloped through the field, while hippopotamus floated in the nearby lagoon. Xavier and Corinne scanned the land, taking note of a family of cheetahs not too far from their position.

"This is beautiful," he said.

Corinne patted the sides of her shorts. "Where's my phone, I have to take a picture of this!"

Xavier chuckled, pulling out her cell phone and handing it over to her.

Corinne peered up at him, and Xavier pushed his mouth to her ear and said, "You left it on top of the counter, when we… um, became distracted."

Corinne giggled and fell to the side in an exuberant laugh. Xavier bit down on his lip with a smile lurking at the corners of his mouth.

"I don't know what you've done to me," Corinne said, "but I've never had this much sex in my life."

Xavier wiggled his brows. "That's good news, baby. I plan to be your first and last all-nighter."

"Slash all-dayer, all-afternooner!" She giggled again, and Xavier nodded.

"Exactly!"

Shaking her head, Corinne lifted her cell phone and captured a few pictures making sure to get the neighborhood giraffes that stood upright eating leaves from a tall mimosa tree. She quickly switched to start a video. In it, she recorded the landscape, animals, and the elephant they sat upon.

"This is awesome," she said, "my parents would love to see this."

"Why don't you show them?"

"I could never get them on the same schedule to come here. My mother's busy with her catering business, and my father is busy with his construction company."

Xavier tapped the phone. "So, show them, on live video."

Corinne smiled. "A-ha!"

She dialed their number and placed the call on video. It rang a few times then Brenda Thomas answered the phone. Her face displayed across the screen while Corinne's sat in the upper righthand corner.

"Hello, my beautiful child, you know your father's been waiting for you to call."

Brenda Thomas's smile held elegance and grace, and her frosted strands of gray hair were pinned to the top of her small head.

"Hey Mom, is Daddy there now?"

"Daniel!" Brenda called.

Corinne could hear his heavy footfalls stomping through the house and seconds later, her phone was filled with his brown aging face.

"Sweet pea," Daniel said. "I thought you had forgotten about us."

Corinne pursed her lips. "You are so dramatic. Listen, I have someone I want you both to meet."

"Who is it?"

"It's someone special, and I didn't want to introduce you this way, but we're together, and I want you to experience something with us real quick."

Corinne glanced over her shoulder, finding Xavier's piercing gaze on her.

"You don't mind, do you?" She whispered.

"Not at all." His profound voice tingled her spine, and she blushed.

"Someone special..." Brenda Thomas oozed. "Well don't keep us in suspense, who is it?"

"I've got an idea," Daniel Thomas responded. He didn't

A Risqué Engagement

sound too pleased about it either. "It's that Valentine you were seen all over the news with making out in that restaurant."

Unease settled in Corinne's stomach, but she shook it off and pushed forward.

"That Valentine is Xavier, and yes, you don't think I'd be making out with just any blow joe off the street, do you?"

"I would hope not," Daniel said. "Although I would've much preferred it if you didn't make out at all until I met the fella."

"Oh, Daddy, do you think you met the guys I made out with in high school?"

"This conversation is not going in a direction that I like," Daniel said.

Brenda pursed her lips tight and tried to contain a hoot that wouldn't be detained, sending her into a fit of laughter.

Daniel scowled at his wife. "I'm sorry, honey, it's funny," Brenda said.

Xavier's face filled the screen next to Corinne's. "Good evening, Mr. and Mrs. Thomas. I'm Xavier Valentine, and I too don't like where this conversation is going."

Corinne pursed her lips, eyed her mother, and they both fell into a round of laughter.

"Okay, okay, look." Corinne waited for her mother's amusement to subside. "Xavier and I are a couple, and I'll be bringing him for dinner um…" she thought for a second. "Scratch that, you'll meet him at Camilla's wedding. I unfortunately don't get any more time off until then."

"Xavier," Daniel said, "Since I don't get to have the"

formal talk with you, I'll just be straight with it. If you hurt my daughter..." he paused. "I'll kill ya."

"Daniel— Dad!" Brenda and Corinne screeched.

Xavier chuckled. "You have my word that I'll take good care of her." Xavier glanced at Corinne. "Always."

Heat gathered in Corinne's cheeks, and she shuffled to change the subject.

"Okay, Mom, Dad, I have something I want you to see." Quickly, Corinne flipped the phone's camera around, and the gasps she heard made her smile.

"Oh, dear heavens, where are you?" Brenda asked.

"We're in Africa!"

"Africa!?" Her parents said concurrently.

"Yeah!"

Corinne continued to move the camera around the area, and with sudden surprise, the elephant moved.

"Ah!" Corinne screeched. "What's happening, oh my God!"

"What is happening?" her parents asked.

Xavier chuckled. "You're okay, we won't go far."

"Are you riding a horse?" Brenda asked.

"No, an elephant!"

Another sharp gasp rang through the phone.

"Corinne Thomas, you get down off that elephant right now, you know there's an ongoing fuss about the safety for that animal!"

Xavier chuckled again. "Like mother, like daughter," he said.

"We're getting down now. I promise she's not hurt, Mama."

Brenda grumbled on the other end.

"That scenery is beautiful. What made you decide to go to Africa?" Daniel asked.

Corinne peered over her shoulder. "Someone special invited me, and I couldn't resist."

Xavier leaned forward and kissed her lips and then her cheek. The mother elephant-headed toward a Riverbed. Once she was there, the mother elephant sank her trunk into the water then tossed it back, splashing Corinne and Xavier.

"Oh my God!" Corinne screeched, and they both laughed harder than they've ever laughed before.

"She's just hot, this is how she cools off!" Phillip the safari guide said, watching them from behind.

"No, she wants you to get off her back," Brenda fussed, glaring through droplets of water that trickled down the phone.

The mother elephant repeated the water toss, but it only made Corinne and Xavier laugh harder.

"Okay! We're sorry!" Corinne yelled. "Come on, babe, let's get down."

The duo laughed as they were sprayed a third time, and eventually, they were helped to the ground. They continued their adventure from the safari truck for the next few hours until they had no choice but to head to their hotel.

Chapter Sixteen

The next two days were complete bliss and surpassed any adventure they'd ever had. Xavier and Corinne found themselves tracking through the exquisite Batoka Gorge with the Victoria waterfall drizzling in the backdrop. They paddled across what was known as the boiling pot in a raft that brought them face to face with the rainfall of water. Then with Xavier's help, they climbed onto a nearby landing of rocks and stood underneath the waterfall.

"Not afraid to get your hair wet, I see," Xavier said as they crossed under the water and were shielded behind it.

Corinne poked her lip out then smiled. "Nope but be warned that you're about to see my hair in its natural state once this is over."

"Hmmm, I'd much prefer it that way."

Corinne twisted her lips. "You lie," she said.

Xavier closed in on her, and Corinne stepped back as he got closer. Her back hit the solidness of the black basalt rock, and her eyes lurched because she knew she was in trouble.

"Now does this look like the face of someone who'd lie to you?"

Xavier grinned naughtily, and Corinne shrieked when he lifted her in his arms. Her legs found their home around his waist and with her comfortable latch came a rigid dragging of his dick to her vagina.

"I've been thinking," Xavier said. His voice was deep and penetrating as he fought to finish his thought through the lava-filled heat that swept over his skin. "What's keeping you in Florida? Everyone you love is either in Tennessee or Illinois."

Corinne practically purred as she responded. "Florida is my home. It's all I've known when it comes to building a foundation. But Chicago is growing on me."

"Then you should stay," he added, "with me."

His dick would not be restricted in his shorts as it reached out and tapped against the seat of her panties.

"Oh…" A moan escaped her lips, and they both instantly became aroused.

"We're in public, we probably shouldn't," Corinne said.

"You're right," Xavier agreed. "We should get out of here before I end up devouring you against this rock."

Corinne's nipples cowered as they hardened. She rotated her hips, causing more heat to balloon in his erection. It became hard as steel, and her fingers trotted down to his shorts, and easily she pulled his bulging member out.

It curved upward and stabbed against her pussy like it had hit a bullseye.

"What are you doing, Bella..." His lips landed against hers for a sweltering kiss.

She spoke between their lips meshing while huffing and puffing. "Getting devoured by you against this rock," she crooned.

Xavier growled and planted her back against the pillar. "Will you stay with me in Chicago?" he asked. "I need you there."

Corinne shuddered. "Yes." Xavier kissed her mouth as Corinne panted again. "Yes," she whispered.

Xavier's heart rocked against his chest. "I don't have a condom," he warned.

They continued kissing as the head of his shaft pierced her mound, threatening to enter her cove.

"I've got my papers," Corinne said. "Do you?"

Xavier pulled off her lips and hovered right over her mouth. With one strong hand, he reached down and slipped her bikini bottom to the side, revealing her precious sanctuary.

"I do," he said, entering her soft and slow.

Corinne's mouth opened, and her head fell back and Xavier rained kisses down her throat. He pushed inside her until not an inch of him was left uncensored. Something like a gurgle bubbled from Corinne's throat, and she wheezed when his hips moved and rotated the sweet juices inside her.

"Fuck..." Xavier's dark voice groveled.

"We're moving forward whenever you guys are ready," a guide said, standing on the opposite side of the water's rain.

"Fuck again," Xavier said, and Corinne giggled then moaned when he rocked inside her core so hard it practically snatched her soul.

Xavier grabbed the back of her neck and pulled her head forward then swallowed her scream as he tore into her pussy, thrust after gutless thrust. Corinne wailed into his throat, and tears sailed from the corners of her eyes at his massive probing and thorough trajectory. His balls clapped the bottom of her ass and a spiral of hot lava coursed through their loins as they fucked to meet each other's orgasm head on. Xavier tried to be quick, but making love to Corinne was a different type of paradise altogether. After what felt like ten minutes but was really twenty, they both came in sync, exploding in a torrent wave of a wet shower. Corinne's crème coursed down Xavier's shaft and he coated not only her walls within but her clean shaven mound. They shook, trembling with a force that had their hearts pounding and their bodies tingling.

Xavier sucked her mouth and ran his tongue down her chin to her neck. He wanted more and felt like an animal now that he'd gotten another taste of her.

"When we get back to the hotel…" He left that sentence in the air, and Corinne nodded in agreement.

"Shall we go back now?" She asked.

"Don't tempt me, woman."

"Okay, how about we head to our next spot and then depending on what's shielding us, try this again."

She couldn't get enough of him either.

"Deal."

He covered her vagina with the thin material of her

bikini bottom and they resurface from behind the falls. From there, their adventure only got better as they found another place to paraglide.

"I can't believe we're doing this here!" Corinne gasped, combing her eyes over the flatlands and hills of Zambia. The land was color-coded and every spot that Corinne's eyes fell upon exciting the adolescent inside of her.

"I told you we would, didn't I?"

"Yeah." Her voice was timid, and they sailed the breeze for as long as possible before landing and being caught up under the big balloon.

"Uh, oh…" Corinne said, seeing the devilish gleam in Xavier's eye.

"Well what do you know, another place for us to hide and…"

Corinne screamed and giggled, and they rolled around finding themselves in another passionate erotic coupling.

When they reached the hotel, Corinne was fast asleep, and Xavier swept her up in his arms and carried her to their room where he laid her on the bed and watched her. His heart swelled as images of Corinne carrying his child began to take shape. He climbed into bed with her and before long was off in dreamland where they both slept through the night and half of the morning into the next afternoon.

When they finally rose, their day started in the shower, and as their last day, Xavier wanted to show Corinne his reasoning for bringing her to Zambia all along. After arriving in a neighborhood filled with children and women carrying buckets of water on their heads and babies on their backs, Corinne gawked and took it all in.

"I've only seen neighborhoods like this in movies," she said.

Xavier nodded. "These families are provided these homes, clean water, and education due to the organizations like Save the Children. They also take donations directly through wire transfer, which helps the most because it gets the money to the people who need it the fastest and most effectively."

"Wow, I didn't know that."

Xavier nodded. Corinne turned to him. "How did you know?"

He rubbed his chin. "I've had my fair share of donating as well, Bella Anima. Would you like to meet the children?"

Corinne's eyes lit up. "Yes!"

They entered the village, and their guide introduced them to the kids and their parents. The kids wore school uniforms and were very lively and joyful. They began doing a ritualistic dance, and Corinne tried to follow their movements. When she felt like she had a few steps down, she asked them to show her again, and they were pleased to do so.

"Mister, do you know how to play ball," one kid asked Xavier.

"By ball you mean basketball?" Xavier asked.

"Yes."

"It's my all-time favorite sport."

The little boy grabbed Xavier's hand. "He plays!" he yelled, and a group of boys crowded him with their own makeshift basketball.

"Oh, you want a piece of me?" Xavier said.

"Yeah!" they shouted.

"All right, let's do this. Now Im'ma go easy on you because I'd hate to embarrass you in front of your friends," Xavier told the first kid that approached him.

The little boy threw Xavier the ball as if to say "check" and Xavier tossed it back. They were playing a game of all of the children against Xavier, running around him in circles, passing the ball back and forth before making their shots in an old rugged hoop.

"Ah, man, ya'll cheating," Xavier said, and the kids all laughed.

On the sidelines, Corinne and the girls did their dance like cheerleaders while the boys played. Some of their movements snagged Xavier's attention as he took his gaze over to the way Corinne's hips rotated. While he was distracted, the ball hit him upside the head, and the group of boys laughed then turned around and sent the ball flying through the hoop.

Corinne and the girls giggled, too, and Xavier winked over at her trying to refocus on the game. Their day was spent at the village, but when it was time to depart, it was bittersweet.

"Visit us again, please!" One little girl begged, tugging on Corinne. Corinne bent down, throwing her arms around the child.

"You have my word."

They embraced with Xavier watching. Again, he thought of Corinne as his bride and mother of his children. He stood by until they finally let go, and with the linking of their fingers, they rode back to the hotel in calmed silence.

Chapter Seventeen

ISLAND HARBOUR, ANGUILLA

*L*ove… for most, it was a myth, a thing not within their reach, the most coveted but priceless antique in human existence. But for some, it was the only thing to strive for, the quintessential belief that one could not survive in this life without it, because well, what was living without affection, passion, caring, fondness, intimacy. Without patience, kindness, faithfulness, and perseverance, life would be, plainly put, bland. Like a constant state of unease. The heart would always want because the thing that keeps it alive would be absent.

There are other ways to find happiness, but these things are temporary, short-lived and require an expiration date. Love is forever, which is why every human being in existence strives to grab hold of it at one time or another. It was why Corinne Thomas laid on her beach towel, soaking up the island sun rays without another singular thought on her mind other than Xavier Valentine. Their trip to Africa was two weeks past them, and since then, Corinne and Xavier shared many nights together, but most of them apart due to their demanding schedules. It only made them yearn for one another more because their singular commonality was love. They were sick with it, so much so that when they couldn't be together, text messages ran thick, video calls were a must, surprise gifts at the most unexpected times arrived.

Just hours ago, before leaving Kinship Airlines, Corinne had been bombarded with a serenading band. They were dressed in island gear and had lit up the airport with their rendition of "The Most Beautiful Girl in The World" by Prince. The elation that bubbled inside her was so strong that her eyes misted over. Xavier had grown accustomed to Corinne's schedule, aware of her layovers like he himself were a part of Kinship Airlines. Corinne understood he was familiar, but still this band and song carried her back to Africa, where he sang to her on his jet, where he serenaded her underneath the waterfall, where he laid his head to rest in the most sensitive part of her flesh. A shiver slipped over Corinne as she recounted their days spent together. No schedule to think of, no emergency to run off to, no one to answer to but each other. It was complete bliss. The kind that sank into her skin and swelled her heart with a tantalizing zing. It was a love she'd never known. One that Corinne didn't think she would one day own. It captivated her with awe and inspired her beliefs that if this thing called love was available to her, surely everyone could attain it.

Corinne sighed. The one thing she regretted was not telling him. It was her wall of defense. Though Xavier had knocked down her barriers regarding men and love, mostly regarding him and love, still Corinne held on to those three words. It was that part of her that wanted to hear him say it first, that part that longed for him to look her in the eye and confess that she was his one true love. It was the thing she coveted, and more than anything else, Corinne needed to know he reciprocated her true feelings. But who says he needed to be the first. Finding out that he'd been hurt by women in the past was enough to give Corinne understanding that loving again for him probably was the hardest relinquished confession that Xavier could make.

Men tended to harbor feelings more than women, at least in her line of love that had been mostly true. So right then and there, with the waves threatening to wash ashore and sweep her back into its aqua blue waters, Corinne decided the next time she saw him, not through video, or through a photo message, but in person, she would let loose and tell Xavier what she desired most. Him.

A smile crept across her face, and she shifted to her back just as a shadow cast over her. Bringing her mind to focus on the darkened change, Corinne's gaze shifted through her shades to find Carlos hovering to the side of her, his silhouette blocking the sunlight.

Corinne lifted her arm and removed her shades. "Carlos?"

"Good evening, Angela," he said, calling her by her alias.

"Good evening, Carlos, how are you today?"

"Better now that you're here."

Corinne chuckled. "How are you better now that I'm here?"

"I've been waiting for you to reappear. I think I must have missed you the last few visits."

Corinne's squinted slightly. "You really think you know my schedule, don't you?"

Carlos's smile didn't give off joy, but more of a leering quirk that Corinne couldn't distinguish as sentimental.

"I do, you're special to me, Angela."

Corinne's laugh was filled with nervousness and uncertainty. She kept nice with him although she began to wonder if she'd have to stop coming to the beach during her layovers here. That would just be unfortunate as Corinne rather enjoyed her time in Anguilla.

"I have something for you," he said.

"Oh?"

Carlos removed a stem from behind his back. It reminded Corinne of the berry plants she used to find in her parents' backyard when she was a child.

"It's called Rondeletia anguillensis. It is a rare Anguilla based plant that only grows on the north side of the island. I thought you should have it since you are also a rare beautiful plant that grows on me every time you visit."

Did he just call me a plant?

"Carlos, that's really sweet, but you truly shouldn't have."

"Yes," Carlos pushed the plant forward, "it is yours please take it."

"I'm sorry, Carlos, I can't take it."

"Yes, you can. Here, it's yours."

Carlos leaned forward then squatted down to offer her the flower, and his nearness freaked Corinne out. She didn't try to, but she scurried just a bit, upon her buttocks now, her hands planted in the sand and her feet backpedaling.

Her response made Carlos frown.

"What is wrong?" He asked.

"Um, nothing!" she said quickly. "I just don't think it's appropriate for me to accept this gift from you. Although lovely, Carlos, my boyfriend would not be pleased."

Carlos frowned.

"You understand, don't you?"

Corinne didn't set out to hurt his feelings, but she needed to let Carlos know in no uncertain terms that anything romantic between them was not in the forecast.

"This is the first time I'm hearing about this boyfriend," he said. "Why?"

The question threw her for a loop. "Um, I… well, it wasn't something that needed to be said before."

Carlos grimaced but didn't respond, only stared at her with an unpleasant narrow to his eyes.

Feeling uneven, Corinne scrambled to her feet. "I'm sorry, Carlos, I really am. We can be island friends, right?" Corinne collected her beach towel, shades, and beach bag as she spoke.

Carlos watched her with the frown continuing to linger on his face.

Corinne cleared her throat. "Anyway, it's time for me to head back. I'll see you next time."

With that, Corinne walked away, her pace fast and her hands rummaging through her bag for the hotel keycard.

She didn't bother glancing back; she could feel Carlos's eyes burning a hole in her back. The walk across the beach seemed like it had taken a few miles, but it was only half of one. The doors opened as she neared the hotel, and she shuffled onto the elevator breathing a sigh of relief once the door closed. *What was that?*

Corinne had always known Carlos flirted with her, but his knowledge of her arrival, and his plans to woo her made her anxious. After locking herself inside the suite, Corinne dropped her bag and strolled to the balcony overlooking the beach. In the distance, she could see the spot she and Carlos had once stood, and her skin crawled when she noticed his form still standing there, seemingly looking right at her. Corinne rubbed her shoulders and tried to shake the unpleasant sensation running through her. He couldn't see her from where he was, could he?

Even she couldn't see the rooms individually while she lay on the beach, so surely he couldn't, right? While she tried to convince herself, unease still crept through her spirit, and suddenly, Corinne couldn't wait to be as far away from Anguilla as possible.

XAVIER LOOSENED HIS TIE AS HE LEFT THE NATIONAL Hockey League headquarters. Today's negotiations had been rough, but nevertheless his quick pro quo had come out to seal the victory. Another million dollar contract negotiated added to his resume and another happy client. Hitting the alarm on his Jaguar, Xavier opened the door and slipped into the driver's seat. He removed his suit jacket and tossed it in the passenger chair and dialed a number on his steering column. The Bluetooth connected, and his seatbelt automatically crossed his chest when the engine roared to life.

"Are you on your way?" Hunter said, answering from the other end.

"Yes."

"So, you *can* get out of a meeting in an orderly time frame. Look at you being all prompt."

Xavier chuckled as he navigated through the streets.

"I find myself being more aware of my time lately."

"Why do I think that has something to do with Corinne?"

Xavier didn't respond immediately. Instead his mind conjured her face, her smile, the deep sexy tone of her laugh.

"I'm pulling up in five minutes," Xavier said.

"I'm inside," Hunter replied.

The call disconnected but rang out before he could shift gears. Xavier tapped the telephone symbol on his steering wheel without checking the caller ID.

"This is Xavier," he smooth voice cruised.

There was a hesitation on the other end then a thick sultry voice broke through the line.

"Xavier, it's been a long time..."

Xavier's attention turned from the road to the caller ID.

"Who is this?"

He kept his tone neutral although he knew very well who the caller was.

She paused again. "Has it been that long that you don't remember my voice."

"I'll ask you again. Who… is this?"

She tried not to feel slighted by his off-put, but she did. Sitting her pierced pride to the side, she returned.

"It's Nadine, Xavier."

Xavier's hands tightened as he steered the car.

"Nadine Benson? As in, the woman I told never to contact me again?"

Suddenly, Nadine thirsted for a bottle of water.

"That was three years ago, I was hoping by now—"

"What? That I would be able to stand your voice or God forbid see your face?"

His language was harsher than necessary, but it was on her. He'd warned her not to reach out to him under any circumstances. Yet here she was, on his line.

"I miss you," she responded. "What we had—"

"Is over," he finished. "And honestly I'm surprised. Didn't Archduke Benjamin Forrest the third teach his little princess not to try and crawl back to any man regardless of the situation? You are royalty after all, nothing or no one supersedes your highness."

"I hurt you," she said. "I understand, and I want to make it right. If you'll just let me."

The phone went dead as Xavier dropped the call and immediately blocked the number. He gritted his teeth and steered the Jag around a corner.

The audacity of Nadine to call as if anything she had to say would be remotely interesting to him. He blew out a breath and shifted his thoughts as he continued to his destination.

Pulling in front of Delaney's Tuxedo shop, Xavier parked the Jag and hopped out. The bell atop the door jingled as he sailed through and was promptly greeted by a member of the staff.

"Mr. Valentine, your party is in the back, let me show you to your space."

Xavier strolled behind the man, appreciative that he'd closed the shop so he and his brothers could be fitted for Hunter's wedding without disturbance.

"There he is," Lance barked as soon as Xavier entered the room. It was an open space with mirrors etched against the wall completely. In this room, you could see yourself in a three hundred and sixty-degree angle, so missing a detail wasn't likely. Xavier slapped hands with Lance.

"That's a nice tux there, brother," Xavier said. "Fits you well. Has it been tailored already?"

Lance nodded as he took a sharp eye over his mirror image.

"Yeah, cuts around my edges just right, too. No tug or rework needed. Almost perfect," Lance said.

"I would leave out almost," Xavier responded, admiring the tux's fit.

Movement in the room caught Xavier's attention, and he crossed the distance to slap hands with Hunter.

"Damn, yours looks equally as sharp."

"That's because it is," Hunter agreed. "Delaney's work is impeccable. It's why we keep coming back for our custom suits."

"Yeah, but I'm surprised you're just now doing this. The wedding is next week. How can you worry your pregnant wife waiting until the last minute to have this done?"

"My pregnant wife doesn't know I waited until the last minute. She thinks I'm here to pick up the tux that I ordered a long time ago."

"I told Corinne you were vile, now look at you being deceptive."

The two men chuckled.

"Nah, not deceptive. I did order this tux weeks ago. I just didn't have the time to get fitted. So I guess I'm a lucky bastard that Delaney's worked with us previously or this would've been a tragedy."

"Could've," Xavier said. "Always stay optimistic, brother."

"Speaking of wives," Hunter began. Xavier arched a prominent brow. "I noticed you ignored my question when we were on the phone."

Xavier knew what question Hunter was referring to, but still he pretended he didn't.

"Which was?"

Hunter smirked, also knowing Xavier knew.

"Would your timeliness have anything to do with Corinne?"

A staff member approached the men then. "Mr. Xavier Valentine, are you ready for your fitting?"

"I am," Xavier said.

Hunter reached out for Xavier's shoulder, stopping him from fleeing this conversation. "Give us a second, Dell," Hunter said.

Dell nodded and Xavier turned back to Hunter. Hunter folded his arms and waited for Xavier's reply. Xavier stood still, musing for a long moment before responding.

"I love her."

Hunter's eyes widened, and a glorious smile cruised across his face. "When did it happen?"

Xavier sighed. "I don't know. I can't explain any of it. Maybe it was our paragliding adventure that did it or the frank way she doesn't kiss my ass just for the sake of doing whatever pleases me. Maybe it's her sincerity and the way she gives and cares for others. Maybe it was Africa or the way she submits herself to me unequivocally. Maybe it was the first time I met her, the feeling I had that she was someone I'd come to call my own." Xavier paused. "Whenever it happened, I'm glad it did. Corinne is truly one of a kind."

Hunter's smile had widened. "I know the feeling," he said, glancing back at himself in the mirror. "Just remember, if you marry her, I introduced you to your wife, so, you owe me one," he teased.

Xavier rubbed his hands together in thought. "Well technically, I helped you save yours, so, we're even."

Hunter's mighty guffaw brought the attention of their other brothers, and Xavier slapped Hunter on the back then pointed at him. "Game, set, match," he said, strolling off to get fitted.

Chapter Eighteen

"Can I talk to you for a minute?"

Corinne glanced at Monica who she'd only spoken to in reference to a task that needed to be handled on board Kinship Airlines.

"Depends," Corinne said. "Is it flight related?"

"Corinne," Monica stepped closer to her, wanting to speak in a lower tone in order to keep the exiting passengers from overhearing their conversation. "I want to apologize. I'm sorry."

Corinne folded her arms and caught an instant attitude. Monica had one chance to keep this conversation on the right road, so Corinne wouldn't tolerate any backhanded compliments or statements regarding her and Xavier's relationship.

"I was out of line when I spoke to you previously about Xavier. I only know what I've seen in the media, and that's an outside looking in type of thing. It wasn't fair for me to judge him without knowing his character. I hope you can accept my apology."

Corinne watched her closely, slowly defrosting at her words.

"I promise it won't happen again. I know I'm pretty closed off most days, and honestly, I hate keeping to myself all the time, I just don't know how else to be." She paused. "Anyway, I hope you have a good weekend, I overheard you talking to Amber about your friend's wedding. Bachelorette parties are always the best parties. At least that's what I've heard since I don't have friends to invite me."

Monica smiled then readjusted her flight uniform blouse. "Anyway, have a good time for me." Monica strolled passed Corinne.

"Monica," Corinne called.

Monica paused and turned back with an inquisitive expression masking her face.

"If you're free, you're more than welcome to join in on the festivities."

Monica's brows arched followed by an elated smile but just as quickly it disappeared. "Oh no, I didn't say all of that for you to feel sorry for me. I really meant—"

"Monica," Corinne cut in. "I don't feel sorry for you," she said frankly. "I've wanted to get to know you better anyway. You just seemed a little bitchy at first, so I also planned to keep to myself." Corinne paused. "However, this bachelorette party could be good for both of us. I'm not going anywhere any time soon. You're not either, right?"

"Right," Monica nodded.

"Then we may as well be friends or at the very least close acquaintances."

Monica smiled brightly and nodded enthusiastically. "You're right. Thank you, I'd love to come."

Corinne smiled. "Good. The party starts tomorrow at seven. If you'd like to ride in the stretch limo with me and the bridesmaids, you're more than welcome to."

Monica clasped her hands together. "That would be fantastic. Here let me give you my number."

Corinne pulled out her cell, and Monica rattled off her phone number.

"What will you be doing in the meantime?" Monica asked.

A risqué smile journeyed across Corinne's lips. "I've got a date with the man of my dreams, but he doesn't know it yet."

"Hmm, sounds like a daring engagement."

Corinne nodded. "I'd say so, but only time will tell."

The two snickered, and they both gathered their things and left the aircraft. On her way to Camilla's apartment, Corinne thought about renting her own space at the luxurious Regency high rise. She had gotten accustomed to the security of the building and the layout of the grand area. It wasn't every day someone could rent from the building as there was an extensive background check, criminal, FBI, and homeland security check because of the tenants living there.

There were athletes, businessmen, politicians, Valentines, but still she would put in an application. Going back to Miami right now didn't appeal to her anymore. She heard Xavier's voice and remembered his words.

"What's keeping you in Florida? Everyone you love is either in Tennessee or Illinois."

"Florida is my home. It's all I've known when it comes to building a foundation. But Chicago is growing on me."

"Then you should stay," he added, "with me."

Snapping out of her thoughts, Corinne entered The Regency and made it to Camilla's apartment without interference. It was a good thing because since she and Xavier had been displayed across every major newspaper in Chicago along with footage of them in the restaurant spinning on some new stations' airwaves, people had been taking random snapshots of her while she was out. At first it was a little weird, but then she realized it came with the territory of being the leading lady in Xavier's life, and if she planned to keep it that way, it would only get worse.

Corinne entered Camilla's apartment and went straight to the guest room. Inside, she headed to the closet where she'd stashed Victoria's Secret lingerie she'd picked up during one of her layovers. She had sworn to save the three-piece set for a night when she and Xavier would have the next few days to roll up under each other, but she didn't want to wait. She was about to turn this evening into a random rendezvous. Swiftly, Corinne's steps carried her to the shower where she lathered herself with an African fragrance he'd gifted her with. The sweet lemon scent seemed to rouse his libido more, so she was sure there was no way for her to go wrong.

As she bathed, Corinne hummed Prince's song with a smile across her face. She rinsed, exited, and lotioned herself from her face down to the crevasses in her feet. She then dressed her thick-a-licious body in the sexy number before adding a spray of her botanical gardens perfume that had her smelling like a fresh lemon orchard. Corinne finger combed her shoulder-length mane, giving it a vixen like bounce as it fell over one eye and cascaded to her shoulders. On her feet, she applied a pair of six-inch razor-like sharp stilettos, then added diamond studs in her ears. She didn't want much jewelry taking away from the way the racy lingerie kissed her body. No, she wanted Xavier to notice how the nude bra looked like skin against her flesh, how the matching open crotch panties practically disappeared into her skin, how the lacy thigh-high pantyhose accented her brown thighs.

After twirling in the full-length mirror, making sure her look was perfect, Corinne grabbed the last piece that would set her look off, a trench coat. She was gone after that, driving down the street with the same tune in her head she'd been singing in the shower. Her mind in one place, determined and set in motion to surprise her man then rock his entire world at the end of his long day of negotiations. She'd checked in with him previously and knew once he left Delaney's Tuxedo shop he would make his way to his office to finalize the deal. So she all but expected to ambush him, in the most glorious way possible. A smile pulled back on Corinne's lips, and she rounded his building before pulling into the underground garage parking lot. She shut the engine off and checked her lip gloss, making sure her mouth still held an immaculate polish.

Feeling perfect, she left the vehicle and her spiked heels hit the cement as her hips twisted in a spicy sashay to the bank of elevators. She entered his key code, the one that would take her straight to the top without any stops. She still hummed as her tongue chased the outline of her teeth. At her destination, the elevator doors opened, and the lounge was empty with only the receptionist at the desk who had her purse on her arm as she prepared to depart for the day.

The receptionist glanced up and did a double take. A smile crossed her face.

"Oh hey, Ms. Thomas, I didn't know Mr. Valentine was expecting anybody else today."

Corinne strolled to her desk. "He's not, this is a surprise, so I would appreciate it, Cynthia, if you kept it to yourself."

"Oh." Cynthia Meadows smiled. "Of course."

"Thank you." Corinne tapped the desk and continued her sashay to Xavier's office. The door was closed, so she knocked twice then entered without waiting to be instructed. To her dismay, Xavier wasn't in his office. It was just as bare as the rest of the workplace. Pursing her lips, Corinne glanced to the wall clock. Maybe he hadn't made it back to the office or maybe he was caught in traffic. Whichever the case may be, Corinne sauntered around the mahogany desk, her fingers dragging along the surface until she made it to his professional leather high-back chair. She whipped it out, then sat with the trench still closed and lifted her legs to prop her feet on the desk edge. She crossed her feet at the ankles and leaned back, causing the chair to tilt slightly on its hydroplane legs. Then she hummed the tune that had been stuck in her head all day and waited for him to arrive.

When the doors to the elevator opened, Xavier stepped out and headed for his office with his thoughts on the surprise he had for Corinne. An elegant smile graced his face. Xavier had managed to pull off many things before, but this one by far was his best surprise yet. He thought of her face and the way she would surely beam when it was revealed, and that warmed his heart to the point where he almost did a fist pump in the air. He was deep in his musing, rounding past his receptionist's desk but was stopped short when someone called out his name.

"Xavier…"

His feet paused and the hair on his neck stood up. He pivoted slowly without revealing his disbelief at the visitor waiting in the seated area. She rose to her feet and slowly made her way up to him, then removed her shades.

"I know you're busy, but can I have your attention for just a minute?"

Xavier didn't respond; instead, he inwardly tried to calm his nerves.

"Please," she said.

"We don't have anything to discuss, Nadine, so, what the fuck are you doing here?"

Nadine Benson locked her jaw then release it and struggled to get her words in order.

"Speak now or forever hold your peace," he said.

"I don't know how many times I can apologize to you."

Xavier let out a frustrated breath.

"You can't be serious?" His voice had grown darker.

"I—"

"We've been over for three years. I don't understand what more there is to say."

"I'm not the woman you think I am."

"You are serious," he said, more annoyed than ever. "Leave."

He turned his back on her and strolled through the building headed for his corner office suite.

Nadine jogged to keep up with his pace.

"I'm not leaving until you give me a chance to say what I have to say!"

Xavier grabbed the doorknob and entered his suite without giving her another word, but Nadine was on his heels, and they both stopped short at the sight of Corinne, now perched on top of his desk with her trench thrown across his chair and her legs crossed over her thighs.

"Hey, baby—"

The sentiment was cut short at the sight of Xavier and Nadine together. Xavier's eyes arched in surprise, and his dick became excruciatingly hard. His eyes dove over her sexy form, and in the same instance, his gaze pitched.

"Shit," Corinne said.

She stood to her feet and didn't hurry to cover herself as she rounded his desk with a sashay in her hips. She grabbed her trench then slid it over her arms and tied the belt tightly. "I didn't realize you would have company so late in the day." Corinne's eyes traveled from Xavier's midnight eyes to Nadine Benson, standing beside him with her mouth hanging open. "Close your mouth, sweetheart, or something may fly in it." Corinne rolled her eyes then rounded the desk again headed for the door.

Xavier moved quickly, reaching out for Corinne before she could make her exit. His hands gripped her arm and pulled her softly but forcefully back over to him. "Now… where do you think you're going?"

Corinne cocked her head to the side. "It appears that you have company." Corinne rolled another eye at Nadine. "I probably shouldn't stay. There's no guarantee that this situation could get better with me around."

She went to move again, but Xavier held her firm.

"Nadine was just leaving," he said, turning around to peer at Nadine. "Isn't that right?"

Nadine finally closed her mouth and blew out a puff of air.

"Xavier."

"Nadine."

"Only if you promise to get in touch with me. I'm not backing down. If you hear me out now, I can get this out of the way."

Corinne sighed behind Xavier, and he turned back to her and sank his fingers between hers. Rounding the desk, Xavier pulled Corinne with him to make sure she didn't escape while he called security.

He lifted the desk phone and hit one button.

"Yes, I have someone here who needs to be escorted out and find out how she got in after hours." Xavier glared up at her as he listened to the security guard. "Yeah, well, when he comes back from the restroom, fire him."

Xavier dropped the phone in its cradle. "You have five seconds."

"I never thought you'd hate me so much," Nadine said.

"I don't hate you. I just don't like you. Now leave. Trust me, it will be more embarrassing to be escorted out."

Nadine huffed then glanced over at Corinne. A smug leer crept across Nadine's mouth. "So, this is what you like, huh," she said. "No class, just all ass."

Corinne's eyes bucked. *Oh, no, she didn't.* "Have you ever had your ass beat by a butt naked woman with no class, Nadine?" Corinne said. "Come here, let me show you." Corinne shook out of Xavier's hands and removed her trench so fast Xavier didn't see it coming. She lurched across the suite, and Xavier reached out to grab her as Nadine recoiled toward the door.

"Let me go!" Corinne shouted.

"Baby, she's not worth it."

"Let me go, Xavier!"

"Bella…"

That seemed to calm her down. The door to the office opened, and security marched in. Xavier made sure to cover Corinne with his front.

"Take her now," he said.

The three guards surrounded Nadine. "Let's go, ma'am."

"Don't touch me!" She shouted.

"If you refuse to leave, we will forcefully remove you."

Nadine swept an eye over at Xavier. "Is this how you operate now, Xavier?" She shook her head. "I thought you were better than this!"

Xavier grabbed Corinne's trench and covered her arms and tied her belt then turned full circle, now covering Corinne with his back.

"It's a shame what happens when we think someone is one way but turns out they're not." Xavier tisked. "I thought you were a lady, but it turns out you're a gold-digging money hungry leech, with no class and no ass." He tisked again.

Nadine flinched at the sting of his words, but he was not done. "And for the record, I don't like this ass, I love it, and wouldn't trade it for anything you had to offer on your best day." Xavier's glare transported to the security guards. "Escort her out now."

The guards closed in on Nadine. Embarrassed, she huffed and spun on her heels then stalked out of the door. It was closed behind the last guard, and without pause, Xavier turned back to Corinne who stood behind him with a smirk on her face. She dropped it instantly and held her chin high in the air.

"What the hell was that?"

"I honestly don't know, and I don't care. I apologize. I never expected to show up and see her here."

Corinne sighed. "She ruined my afternoon gift to you."

Xavier's brawny hands slipped up her shoulders to her neck.

"Maybe, maybe not." He grinned. "You know, you're a very bad girl for showing up here like this."

Corinne smirked. "I know, that was the whole purpose."

Xavier's hands trod down the jacket to untie the knot in the belt.

"We should start over," he said, removing the trench from her shoulders. "Damn." His eyes combed over her physique, and he bit his bottom lip then released it. Corinne leaned in and kissed the beard surrounding his chin. Then his lips. She stepped out of his arms and let the trench fall then turned around and gave him her best pinup model pose. Xavier reached out and smacked her ass, causing it to bounce off the palm of his hand.

"Oooh…" she purred.

"Come over here, let me show you something," he said, leading her to his desk. He bent her over, squatted on his haunches, then stuck his face between her ass.

"Aaaaah!" she squealed.

His tongue whipped against the highway of her derriere then sank into the plush softness of her pussy.

"Oh God…" Corinne moaned bending over further to spread her peach wider.

A dark moan fled from Xavier, and his brawny hands latched onto her hips. He sank to his taut ass, then spread out on his back keeping Corinne's mound stuffed on top of his mouth.

She was riding his face now, with her head thrown back and her hips bucking and thrashing her pussy over his tongue.

"Oh my God, I'm going to come so hard," she squealed.

It was in her intentions to fall forward and removed his dick for her own greedy undertaking. But the lashing Xavier whipped against her vagina weakened Corinne in an instant and she came spurting crème all over his mouth.

"Aaah! Oh my God!"

Xavier covered her plum with sweet torture and sucked her dry. When he was done, he flipped Corinne over and lifted her with ease, stalking over to the chaise lounge in the corner of the room.

"Oh dear Heaven!" Corinne screamed as the spread of her womb opened to receive him. "Oh... oh... oh..."

Xavier submerged himself entirely, wrapping his hand around the span of her neck and ricocheting off her ass in a vibrant spring that had them both cursing and praising one another at the same time.

It was a beautiful beat down as their juices flowed and their bodies joined in a dance that held them captive and howling like wounded animals. When it was time for their release, Xavier's hands created a molded fingerprint on her side as he volleyed and pounded her sweet heat so hard that their levees broke simultaneously.

"Aaaah!" Corinne screamed, and Xavier sank his teeth into her neck piercing her skin with a forceful sting.

A wave of tremors flowed through them, and their orgasm fell as they held each other tight clinging together as if any sudden movement would end their life.

Chapter Nineteen

"Why are you sitting over there with that smile on your face?" Camilla asked Corinne.

It was Saturday night, and they were at Camilla's bachelorette venue, a night-club that they'd rented out. The party was in full swing, with dessert tables, wine, champagne, and of course sparkling cider for Camilla since she couldn't drink any alcohol.

"It must be Xavier," Camilla concluded when Corinne didn't respond.

Corinne gave off a dreamy sigh, her thoughts still with Xavier the day before. Not only had he rocked her world all over that entire suite, but he gobbled her down like there was no food left to man—except her.

"Girl, I'm not even going to share. It would be rude and probably make a few of you hussies jealous."

Camilla gawked as did the others, and Corinne laughed.

They were accompanied by Monica, Allison, London, and a few other ladies from Camilla's workplace.

"Oh, I'm not jealous of you by far," Camilla said.

"Well, maybe not you, but these others hussies would be."

"Yeah, you're right. Keep it to yourself," Allison said.

Allison Sullivan was the assignment editor over at WTZB. She and Camilla had become friends during Camilla's transition from Miami to Chicago. Now she and Corinne were also good friends, so it only made sense for them to all be together. Besides that, Allison had her eye on Lance Valentine and vice versa, but she wasn't one to believe that their friendship would go much further than the occasional phone calls they'd had thus far. That was one of the reasons she didn't want to hear about Corinne's escapade. She didn't want to give envy a chance to wiggle its way into her spirit.

The lights dimmed and a beat dropped, then the disco bulbs hanging from the ceiling cast a multilayer of colors in one spot on the stage.

"Ouuu! You know what that means," Corinne said, happy to change the subject.

"Oh my God, I told you guys not to go overboard," Camilla said. She glanced around at all of them.

"Don't blame me. I didn't have anything to do with it. I was just recently invited."

It was London Jones who'd spoken. After leaving the meeting with the Valentines and the Roses, London had run into Camilla also leaving the building. With an unfamiliar face before her, Camilla had asked London who she was looking for.

"Oh, I'm with the Roses. I'm London Jones, their caregiver."

At Camilla's arched brow, London reiterated. "I mean, not the Roses' caregiver. I take care of one of the mothers-in-law." She laughed nervously. "Anyway, I'm headed out."

London turned to leave.

"What a minute," Camilla said. "I'm Camilla Augustina."

London's surprise was shown on her face. "Oh, you're the bride to be. Congratulations." London held out her hand, and Camilla accepted with a smile.

"Thank you." Camilla thought about her next proposal and felt inclined to go forward with it. "Listen, London, I'm not supposed to be here, but I had to stop by for a second. I'm actually on my way to lunch with a friend. If you'd like to join us, you're more than welcome, too."

Camilla knew the Valentines and the Roses were at odds, but in her opinion, it was nonsense, all male egos at play. If she could bring the power families together, they could both really make a difference in Chicago. Not that they weren't now, but they were so busy fighting that they couldn't see the potential. As the future Mrs. Valentine, Camilla felt compelled to do something, even if it was as small as having London enter their circle. Besides, London seemed harmless enough; she might even make a good ally.

"Oh no, I can't. I have Ms. Stevens in the car, but thank you anyway."

London went to leave again and was stopped a second time.

"London!" Camilla's voice elevated. London turned back. "Are you off on Saturdays?"

London nodded. "Yeah, why?"

A smile eased across Camilla's face. "How do you feel about bachelorette parties?"

From there, Camilla and London exchanged information, and now, London was among the crew at Jazzy's night-club.

Allison stood to her feet. "Okay, Camilla, let's go, you know how this works, don't you?"

"Oh my God…" Camilla whined, standing to her feet. She was wearing a head crown with a bridal veil hanging from the back and a one piece all white body-hugging floral dress. On her feet, all-white Christian Louboutins. Allison grabbed her hand, and they sashayed up to the stage.

Corinne shook her head and laughed then took out her camera phone.

"This I have to get on video," she said.

After helping Camilla to her seat, Allison moved from the stage when three muscled men in police gear strutted out on the stage.

"Ouuuuu!" Corinne shouted.

"Oh my God, my husband is going to kill ya'll!" Camilla shouted.

"Girl, the only one seeing this video is us. Your husband will never know."

The men danced up to Camilla and gyrated around her in circles.

"Whew!" Camilla exclaimed.

"Unhuh, acting like you don't like it," Corinne said from the front of the stage. She held her phone up as she recorded and laughed out loud with her tongue hanging out at the way they rubbed their third leg around her from all sides.

"Good lawd!" London said.

And the others howled with laughter.

"This is better than I could've ever imagined," Allison added.

"Yes, yes!" Corinne agreed. Her video call was interrupted by a phone call. "Unknown number?" she muttered. "Here we go with this."

"Hello," Corinne answered.

"Hello, may I…"

"Hello, I can't hear you, who's this?"

The person on the other end tried to speak again, but there was static on the line, and Corinne could hardly hear with the music in the background of the club.

"Hold on for a minute let me find a quiet spot."

Corinne slipped away from the girls, and Allison yelled over her shoulder.

"Where are you going, you're supposed to be recording!"

"I'll be back, take over for me."

Corinne slipped through the tables and strolled down a long corridor to enter the women's restroom. Although the club had been rented out, the building was a two-story industrial size structure. So where it was rented out on the second floor, the first floor was popping with party goers in a completely different layout.

"Hello," Corinne shouted into the phone. The bathroom was empty, and she strolled to the sink to check her reflection in the mirror. "Hello? If you don't say something, I'm hanging up now, who is this?"

Silence.

Corinne disconnected the call and sighed in frustration.

"Somebody's trying to get me all worked up," she spoke to herself in the mirror. "But you're looking fierce, girl." She turned from side to side to check her curves in the halter top and thigh-high skirt. The necklace around her neck read "Bride Squad." She took her fingers over the arcs in the emblem. Swooping her hair to the side of her neck, Corinne rubbed her lips together and took an eye over the perfection of her foundation. "Excellent," she said.

Corinne pulled her cell back to her face and scrolled through her call log. Unknown number, she read. Shrugging, she tucked the phone into her palm then walked across the vinyl floor and pushed through the bathroom doors to exit, running into the solid wall of a man's chest.

"Oh my goodness, I'm sorry, I didn't realize anyone was coming in…" Her eyes traveled up his island shirt and enlarged when they reached his face. "Carlos?!"

Carlos's smile was eerie just like it had been the last time she'd seen him in Anguilla.

"Good evening, Corinne," he said.

"What— what're you doing here?" She asked, bewildered, but after the question left her lips, Corinne realized he'd called her by her government name. She took a step back.

"What's going on, Carlos?" She tried not to show fear, but it was written more so in her voice than it was on her face.

"My name is not Carlos. Just like your name is not Angela."

Corinne's mouth went dry, and she glanced around quickly before bringing her eyes back to him.

"No one's coming this way. I made sure of it before I came down the hall."

A foreboding crept over Corinne. "What do you want?"

Carlos cocked his head to the side. "Isn't it obvious? I want what I've always wanted. You."

Carlos's hand rose and the gleam from the gun in his hand caught her attention. Corinne gasped sharply.

"You would fare well not to scream. I don't have a problem hurting the others if I need to, but I only came here for you."

"Please, I don't know what I did for you to—"

"Ssssh…" He put his finger to her lip, and Corinne fought the instinct to bite it off. "Come with me." He nodded toward the elevator shaft, and Corinne hesitated then glanced back down the corridor. "Don't," Carlos said. Reluctantly, Corinne stepped in front of him and boarded with no other choice.

Chapter Twenty

TWENTY MINUTES EARLIER

Robed in a scantily clad dress, Amelia carried the tray of Brandy to the table surrounded by the gorgeous Valentine men.

"On the rocks," she said, bending over to make sure all of her assets were on full presentation.

"Thank you," the men said. One by one, they grabbed their glasses, and Amelia proposed an offer she was sure they couldn't refuse.

"If you need anything else," her eyes were directed at Hunter, then Xavier, then Lance, "anything at all, your wish is my command." She winked, swiped her tongue across her lips, then turned and sashayed away.

"Damn, I think she wanted to take the three of you on at once. A girl like that must have some superwoman pussy."

The men laughed at Devon, the COO of VFC Energy. He along with the Valentine men and a few of their close acquaintances were parked at the Rouge, a gentleman's club uptown not far from Jazzy's.

"I'm serious," Devon went on, "if she comes back by, you should at least tip the girl."

"I don't think she wants a tip," Lance said.

"Are you inclined to give her what she wants, brother?" Hunter asked.

"Are you?" Lance countered.

Hunter pulled out a stack of ones. "This is all I have for her."

The men chuckled. "How about you, X, you're awfully quiet over there."

Xavier pulled the glass of Brandy to his lips and took a sip.

"I think I'm gonna get out of here." He rose to his feet.

"Where are you going?" Devon asked.

"You just can't wait, can you?" Hunter said.

A smirk filtered Xavier's lips. "Nah, you know how it is."

"You lucky bastard," Hunter said.

"But you're the lucky one, brother. You get to spend your life with your wife and your forever starts tomorrow."

"Yeah, but tomorrow isn't promised," Hunter said.

The words echoed in the back of Xavier's mind, and he reached out and slapped hands with Hunter.

"You're right, so forgive me if I cut and run."

Hunter nodded. "No hard feelings just don't come knocking at my door for the next month."

A thunderous round of laughs ran around the room.

"Poor Camilla," Devon said, "she won't be able to walk for weeks after this bastard is done with her."

"Hey," Hunter said, "watch your mouth, don't talk about my wife that way."

Devon raised his hands in surrender. "Don't shoot the messenger."

The men guffawed, and Xavier shook his head and left the building. He jumped in his Jaguar and headed down the avenue. On his way to Jazzy's, Xavier could only hope that Corinne wouldn't be upset with him for interrupting her night. The need to be with her had become an addiction that he could no longer deny. As he passed under the street lamps, Hunter's parting words stuck out in Xavier's mind.

"Yeah, but tomorrow isn't promised."

Xavier reached for his phone, suddenly having the urge to call and connect with Corinne. With his device in hand, he flipped it over and over in the palm of his hand as he wheeled the luxury vehicle with the other. A part of him wanted to surprise her and whisk her away into the middle of the night, but there was another part of him that felt strange, and he couldn't shake the uncanny feeling he had.

Turning on East Delaware, Xavier cruised the Jag around the lounge of Jazzy's, pausing the rotating of his phone to dial a number. He waited for the Bluetooth to connect, when it did, music could be heard in the background and a man's voice shouted through the phone.

"Hey, Xavier, what's going on, man!"

"Paul, I'm circling the building, and I need to get to the second floor. Open the back door and let me in."

"Aw man, you know that door is for emergencies only."

"This is an emergency."

"How's that?"

"I don't want to get bombarded trying to get to my woman. Now open the damn door, Paul."

Paul laughed. "Come on, man, getting a little attention couldn't be so bad! Besides, I'd love to introduce you tonight. I'd have a packed house every weekend if word spread that the Valentines partied here!"

Xavier shook his head. "Another time, Paul. Open the door."

"Aw, man, come on!"

"I'm pulling to the exit now. Come down."

"I can open it from where I am with the push of a button. Oh, I didn't tell you! This place is loaded now. There are no guards at the door because my security system is top of the line."

"Yeah, what happens when your crowd gets out of hand?"

"I didn't say I didn't have guards, they just aren't at the door."

"So, who is?"

"No one, but I never leave the screens unmonitored for long. The door is open, and I've already left the security room."

"You should never leave them period."

Don't worry about it. My backup man will be in there in no time."

Xavier shut off his engine and pulled his long legs out of the car. He slammed the door. "All right, appreciate you, later."

"Aye don't be a stranger, man."

"I won't."

Xavier ended the call and strode across the brick alleyway to the back door. He reached for the handle and opened it, coming face to face with Carlos and Corinne. His immediate response was surprised as his brows lifted and a smile began to form, but when his eyes shuffled between the despair on Corinne's face and the scowl on Carlos's, the smile dropped, and his face drew into a dark mask.

"Bella…"

Corinne shook her head, and her gaze motioned to Carlos's hand that was pinned in her side. Xavier glanced down and spotted the revolver and Carlos waved it at Xavier then back at Corinne.

"Don't think about doing something stupid," Carlos said.

Xavier's dark gaze held firm on Carlos. "I don't know who you are, and frankly I don't care," Xavier said. "But if you think you're getting past me with my woman, think again." His voice was ominous, his adrenaline already pumping at an all-time high.

Carlos squinted and sneered. "Oh yeah, who's going to stop me? You?" Carlos moved his hand up, pointing the gun at Corinne's head. "I'd blow her away before you got the chance to—"

On instinct, Xavier moved, slamming his fist into Carlos's face. The force of his hit knocked Carlos off Corinne, and Xavier reached for her, snatching Corinne so fast it felt like a half a second between the movement. He shielded Corinne behind his back as a battlefield cry shrieked from Carlos and simultaneously blood spurted from his nose.

Carlos lifted the gun again just as Xavier reached for the weapon, grabbing it around its barrel. The two wrestled over it for a long second when a shot rang out once, then twice. Xavier gained the upper hand, twisting Carlos's wrist so hard it snapped.

"Aaaaaaaaaaah!" Carlos screamed.

Another blow to Carlos's face took him down, then another, and finally a stomp to his abdomen.

"Aaaaah! Fuck! Son of a bitch!" Carlos screamed.

Xavier reached for the gun and lifted it over Carlos.

"Xavier!" Corinne shouted. "Don't, baby, please!"

Xavier's aim held firm; he had a clear shot that would send Carlos to meet his maker. Hunter's words reverberated in his head.

"Yeah, but tomorrow isn't promised."

And Xavier realized how close he'd come to possibly losing Corinne forever. What if he hadn't been there? What if he'd decided to stay at the bachelor party and let Corinne enjoy her night with the ladies? In that moment, he'd gone mad, and his finger began to close around the trigger.

"Xavier!" Corinne screamed. "Please, I need you, baby please!"

In an instant, her words pulled him from his thoughts, and he turned to her just as a bounty of security enclosed around them. Xavier dropped the gun and pulled Corinne into his arms.

"Are you hurt!?" His deep voice throttled over her skin. His hands felt around her, checking every inch of every spot on her body.

Corinne trembled and grabbed hold to his shirt where she clutched him tightly, never wanting to let him go.

"I'm fine. I think." She was shell-shocked, and the commotion around them doubled than tripled as police entered the area.

"Xavier!" Paul called out, jogging down the corridor.

Xavier stuffed his face into Corinne's hair and held her tight as his heart knocked just as hard as hers. He locked his jaw and closed his eyes, grasping her so firmly it would take the Jaws of Life to separate them.

Corinne stuffed her face into his chest. "I'm sorry," she said, her words muffled as she sniffled.

Xavier's hands rounded to her face, and he lifted her chin.

"Bella, you have no reason to be sorry," he said, his heart tight at the thought that she could possibly blame herself for what had just taken place.

Corinne nodded. "I—" she stuttered. "I know him."

Xavier frowned. "Who is he?"

"Carlos, the guy from Anguilla." Tears flowed down Corinne's face. "He knew my name. He's been stalking me." An outpour of tears flooded her cheeks, and Xavier drew her face into his and kissed every spot that was wet.

"This is not your fault." He kissed her lips. "I don't care how you knew him or what you said. It is never a fault of your own when someone sets out to stalk you or do you harm." He kissed her so hungrily his heart felt like it would explode from the love and desire that filled him.

Corinne's tears continued to flow, and her heart was mixed with several emotions. Among them was guilt, but what overtook her at that moment was love. An indescribable feeling that she'd never felt before and couldn't explain.

"I love you," Xavier said between kisses.

That just made Corinne cry harder but happy tears this round.

"I love you, too," she said, and their tongues tied as their lips sealed in a scorching kiss.

Chapter Twenty-One

SUNDAY MORNING

New Life Tabernacle Apostolic Church

EVEN THOUGH CORINNE WAS ONLY A FEW FEET AWAY FROM him as she stood behind the bride, Xavier still felt naked without her on his arm. Last night had been the craziest night of his life. He'd witnessed a real phenomenon, and it had nothing to do with Corinne's stalker Carlos. Xavier stared at Corinne from behind his best man's position aside Hunter, and although he heard the vows his brother spoke, in Xavier's mind it was his words with Corinne on the receiving end. Never in a million years would he have recognized himself in this position; with wanting to love someone for eternity like he desired with Corinne.

He was sure after Nadine, that wouldn't happen, not a chance in hell. But fate had something entirely different in his stars, and it settled in his heart and spiraled through him like an enchanted spell. Xavier was in love, and his forever stood so close he could taste her... again. After leaving the club last night, he'd placed her in the safety of his car and asked, "Come home with me, please."

"You don't have to ask, just take me with you," she responded.

It was his pleasure. After speaking to the owner of Jazzy's, the police, and updating everyone at the bridal and bachelor parties, the two never left each other's side, showering together and locking around each other limb to limb throughout the night. It was ecstasy, but at the same time, last night's events made Xavier realize that life was short. Hunter was right, tomorrow isnt not promised, so he wanted to make sure Corinne knew just how much he loved her with every moment they breathed.

"I do."

The sanctuary went up in applause and a thunderous stomping after Hunter spoke those words. Xavier pulled from his musings and slapped a firm hand against Hunter's shoulder.

Tears ran down Camilla's face as she repeated his declaration.

"I do," she said.

Another round of stomping coursed through the building, and some of the bridesmaids shouted beside her garnering a laugh from Camilla and Hunter.

"By the power invested in me, I now pronounce you Mr. and Mrs. Valentine."

The applause was deafening. Hunter lifted Camilla's veil and slipped his hands to her neck, pulling her in for a mouthwatering kiss. The crowd had gone so wild that the building shook, and the bride and groom turned together and side by side took a bow.

When they took their walk down the aisle, celebratory confetti was thrown at them, and the couple made their exit hand in hand. Coming to also stand by each other's side, Xavier and Corinne held a loving eye on one another. Xavier lifted his arm and Corinne slipped hers through.

"I know this is Hunter and Camilla's wedding, but I have something for you."

Corinne arched a brow. "A gift?"

Xavier rubbed his beard with one hand. "Of sorts," he said. I can't really call it a gift."

Corinne was intrigued.

"You'll see what I mean."

"Where is this non-gift?"

Xavier chuckled. "At the reception." He motioned toward the exit. "Shall we?"

Corinne smiled and nodded, then the two headed for the soiree.

"I'D LIKE TO PROPOSE A TOAST." XAVIER STOOD TO HIS feet and cast a glance around the expensively decorated room. "To the bride and groom." The attendees repeated after him.

"To the bride and groom!"

Xavier went on. "May you have more love than you can possibly contain." He glanced at Camilla. "Camilla, you're a great addition to this family, and I couldn't be happier to have you as a sister. You and Hunter will take the world by storm and become a bigger power couple than Beyoncé and Jay-Z."

A round of laughter cruised around the room, and Camilla and Hunter smiled and laughed with them.

"Thank you!" Camilla said. "I guess I can now call you brother."

They laughed again, noting that the Valentines didn't call each other by name but referred to one another as "brother."

"On that note," Xavier said, glancing to Hunter, "brother, it's not every day that you find the woman of your dreams." Hunter nodded. "And you truly have a gem in Camilla Augustina Valentine." Snickers went about, and Camilla interrupted him.

"Drop the Augustina, it's just Valentine baby!"

Another round of rambunctious laughter coursed throughout, and Hunter leaned over to kiss Camilla's cheek. She blushed, and whistles carried throughout the room.

"You've got me there, I stand corrected," Xavier said. "Congratulations to you both." He took his eye across the table where the bridesmaids sat, particularly to Corinne Thomas. "You know, last night, Hunter, you said something that stuck with me and haunted me all through the night." Corinne's expression turned quizzical as Xavier glanced between her and Hunter.

"What was that, brother?" Hunter asked.

"Tomorrow isn't promised." Xavier paused and Hunter nodded, remembering the conversation. "You were right." Xavier's chest tightened as he thought about what he'd shown up to the club to witness, and his gaze sauntered back to Corinne.

"Bella… a month ago I'd spoken with you on the phone. At the time, I felt an urgency so great to be with you that I asked you to meet me halfway between where you are and where I am, right now." Corinne smiled, recalling the request. "I was determined to get to you, but you were in Anguilla, and there wasn't a logical way for us to come together in a timely manner." He cleared his throat. "I didn't know it then, but I know now that I've loved you from the very moment we met."

Corinne's eyes lurched, and she gasped along with everyone else in the room.

Xavier glanced around to her parents, Brenda and Daniel Thomas, who he'd had a lengthy conversation with before making the toast, then his gaze traveled back to Corinne. "I know, sounds impossible, right?" he chuckled. "Well I'm here to tell you, that nothing's impossible when it comes to the matters of the heart. And I'm here to ask you again, baby, if you will meet me halfway between where you are and where I am right now."

All eyes turned to Corinne, and her heart tumbled in her

chest. She blinked and rose to her feet, the chair behind her scrapping across the floor. As she moved, so did Xavier, and everyone watched on as they met in the center of the floor.

"There's something in my pocket I've been dying to get out." He gripped her hands and went down on bended knee.

Corinne's eyes widened, and her mouth opened. "Xavier!" she screamed, her nerves rattled before he could ask her the ultimate question.

"Bella Anima, will you do me this honor and spend the rest of your days, afternoons, and nights with me?"

The ring he removed was in a gold box and when it opened, a glimmer cruised through the princess cut.

"Oh my God, yes!" she shouted. Tears ran down the corners of her eyes, and Xavier stood and lifted her into his arms. He twirled her, and their faces mashed as their lips joined in a hot titanium kiss.

The building rattled as the thunderous applause shook the structure and Xavier squeezed Corinne tight slowly sitting her to her feet. She squealed as he put on the ring and a voice nearby cut into their celebration.

"Congratulations."

Corinne turned to the person who'd spoken. The young girl's face held familiarity, but Corinne couldn't pin it.

"I hope you don't mind me joining your festivity." Her voice held a deep accent. "But I wanted to introduce myself. I've been waiting a long time to meet you."

Corinne glanced at Xavier who held her with a resplendent grin.

"Who are you?"

"Natasha Kaweme," she said.

Corinne's mouth dropped, and a rush of tears streamed down her cheeks.

"You're kidding!"

Natasha smiled. "I'm afraid I am not."

Corinne glanced back at Xavier, her mouth open unable to take in a breath properly. Looking back at Natasha, Corinne threw her arms around the girl and hugged her so tightly she could feel Natasha's heartbeat. Laughter poured from their mouths, and tears mixed on their shoulders as they embraced.

When Corinne pulled back, she stared at the face of the girl she sponsored long ago. She was still young, possibly early twenties, but it was her face nonetheless.

"I wanted to let you know," Natasha began, "that your donations help feed my family and me. I also had a chance to go to school and now I'm a missionary, traveling the globe to help others. So I just want to say thank you so much. You are like my second mother."

Corinne cried so hard she could've fainted. She couldn't even respond, only pull Natasha back in while reaching for Xavier. The three of them hugged so tight it was scorching, and everyone who looked on also held tears in their eyes.

"Thank you so much," Corinne cried, speaking to Xavier. "You have no idea how much this means to me." Her voice trembled, and Xavier tightened his grip.

"I love you," he said, "and I wanted you to know that your uncle Bennie is an asshole."

Corinne shouted out a laugh and tittered to the side. Xavier looked at Natasha. "We would love it if you could stick around for a while, even if it's just to catch this live band."

Corinne peered at him, and Natasha nodded, saying, "I'd love to!"

Xavier kissed Corinne on her temple then released them both and walked to the stage. When Hunter, Lance, and DeAndre followed, everyone moved forward to hear them play. Corinne threw her head back and laughed again before grabbing hold of Natasha as they rejoiced in watching A Band of Brothers serenade them all.

The End

DID YOU ENJOY *A RISQUÉ ENGAGEMENT*? SUBSCRIBE TO MY newsletter or join my Facebook Group to get updates from me, the author! Stay tuned for the pre-order on the next installment featuring Lance Valentine and Allison Sullivan in: *Give Me a Reason*.

Connect with Me on Facebook!
Connect with Me on Instagram!

Note from the Author

THANK YOU SO MUCH FOR READING *A RISQUÉ Engagement,* In the Heart of a Valentine, book two. I hope you enjoyed Xavier and Corrine's story! Reviews are the lifeblood of independent writers. The more reviews we get, the more Amazon and others promote the book. If you want to see more books by me, Stephanie Nicole Norris, a review would let me know that you're enjoying the series. If you liked the book, I ask you to write a review on Amazon.com, Goodreads, or wherever you go for your book information. Thank you so much. Doing so means a lot to me.

2018 Author Sightings!

XOXO - Stephanie

Other Books by Stephanie Nicole Norris

Contemporary Romance

- Everything I Always Wanted (A Friends to Lovers Romance)
- Safe with Me (Falling for a Rose Book One)
- Enough (Falling for a Rose Book Two)
- Only If You Dare (Falling for a Rose Book Three)
- Fever (Falling for a Rose Book Four)
- A Lifetime with You (Falling for a Rose Book Five)
- She said Yes (Falling for a Rose Holiday Edition Book Six)
- Mine (Falling for a Rose Book Seven)
- The Sweetest Surrender (Falling for a Rose Book Eight)
- No Holds Barred (In the Heart of a Valentine Book One)

Romantic Suspense Thrillers

- Beautiful Assassin
- Beautiful Assassin 2 Revelations
- Mistaken Identity

- Trouble in Paradise
- Vengeful Intentions (Trouble in Paradise 2)
- For Better and Worse (Trouble in Paradise 3)
- Until My Last Breath (Trouble in Paradise 4)

Christian Romantic Suspense

- Broken
- Reckless Reloaded

Crime Fiction

- Prowl
- Prowl 2
- Hidden

Fantasy

- Golden (Rapunzel's F'd Up Fairytale)

Non-Fiction

- Against All Odds (Surviving the Neonatal Intensive Care Unit) *Non-Fiction

About the Author

Stephanie Nicole Norris is an author from Chattanooga, Tennessee, with a humble beginning. She was raised with six siblings by her mother Jessica Ward. Always being a lover of reading, during Stephanie's teenage years, her joy was running to the bookmobile to read stories by R. L. Stine.

After becoming a young adult, her love for romance sparked, leaving her captivated by heroes and heroines alike. With a big imagination and a creative heart, Stephanie penned her first novel *Trouble in Paradise* and self-published it in 2012. Her debut novel turned into a four-book series packed with romance, drama, and suspense. As a prolific writer, Stephanie's catalog continues to grow. Her books can be found on her website and Amazon. Stephanie is inspired by the likes of Donna Hill, Eric Jerome Dickey, Jackie Collins, and more. She currently resides in Tennessee with her husband and two-year-old son.

https://stephanienicolenorris.com/

CPSIA information can be obtained
at www.ICGtesting.com
Printed in the USA
LVHW082112121118
596842LV00015B/383/P